PRAISE for S
(Book 1 in the Winston Wong mystery series)

*"Seniors Sleuth* is a delightful whodunit filled with colorful senior citizens, numerous red herrings, and even a little dash of romance for our earnest rookie investigator, Winston Wong. A charming cozy debut that will keep you guessing until the very end."
> —Sarah M. Chen, author of "Canyon Ladies" in the Sisters in Crime/LA's anthology, *LAdies Night*

"J.J. Chow entices mystery readers with her fledgling 'senior' detective. Winston Wong finds himself sought out by aging baby-boomers because of a typo in his *Pennysaver* ad. Luckily his first client has a stunning granddaughter and he needs the money. What follows is more than Winston bargained for—a murder investigation at the Sweet Breeze Care Facility. Winston's love of video games aids him in pursuing the truth about Joseph Sawyer's death and the author's clear, precise prose puts the reader into the story fast and carries through to the end."
> —Gay Degani, author of the literary suspense, *What Came Before*

"Winston Wong is not your conventional private detective. For a start, he's a video game nerd and on the wrong side of forty with very few prospects on the romance front. Not only that, Winston's first case investigating the demise of a ninety-year-old man looks like a non-starter. But Winston is determined to make a success of his new career and soon discovers that it's not just death that roams the corridors of Sweet Breeze retirement home.

"Chow's work in geriatric welfare provides an intriguing backdrop that she skillfully weaves into her clever plot. *Seniors Sleuth* is written with warmth, humor, and an eccentric cast of characters and, most of all, a loveable hero. It's a breath of fresh air to what I hope will become a continuing series."
> —Hannah Dennison, author of the Honeychurch Hall

mysteries and the Vicky Hill mysteries

"Winston Wong, a slacker game developer in the middle of Silicon Valley, is a completely charming rookie sleuth. His modern high-tech world intersects the old, as Winston finds himself embroiled in a suspicious death at a senior home. J.J. Chow adds a fresh, original voice to the mystery genre! I can't wait to read more of Winston's adventures."

—Naomi Hirahara, Edgar Award-winning author of the Mas Arai and Officer Ellie Rush mysteries

"*Seniors Sleuth* is a charming, humorous novel with an intriguing storyline wrapped with endearing characters. It's a total enjoyment to read."

—Lois Lavrisa, bestselling award-winning author of *Dying for Dinner Rolls*

# ROBOT REVENGE

*a Winston Wong mystery*

J.J. Chow

Cover design by Heena Thombre
Edited by Linda G. Hatton

# CHAPTER 1

WINSTON REACHED INSIDE the small red velvet bag and pulled out its precious contents. One by one, he laid out the jewel-toned dice, arranging them by size: the regular six-sided ones all the way to up to the twenty-faced icosahedrons. He didn't know what he'd need for this evening's date night.

The doorbell rang right on time, and he jumped up to let Kristy in. She'd changed out of her usual working scrubs and into something more comfortable—a soft knit turtleneck with gray slacks. They'd been dating a while, but he still couldn't believe his good luck on meeting her at the Sweet Breeze senior home during his first case.

Kristy smiled at him, her deep-brown eyes gazing into his. "Well, are you going to let me in?"

"Sorry." Winston moved aside. "Still getting used to our D&D nights."

"What's the adventure this time?" she asked as she stepped into the living room. He'd hidden the usual clutter in the "storage" bedroom and even wiped down the glass-top coffee table for her visit.

"I need to consult the book," he confessed as he closed the front door. He'd played lots of Dungeons & Dragons as a kid, but he still needed to follow the manual to make up a quest. His older sister, Marcy, had been the Dungeon Master during his childhood.

The tea kettle whistled in the kitchen, and Winston hurried to get it. He'd made some pumpkin spice chai in honor of the fall season. Even though it was autumn, he'd left the kitchen door propped open to bring in the breeze. It was a warm evening—or maybe he was just uber excited.

When he returned to the room, he carried in some chipped mugs—freebies from the video game companies he'd tested for. Kristy was already settled on the couch and had rearranged the throw pillows. Actually, she'd bought him the new velvet cushions to make sitting more comfortable. She patted the empty space next to her.

He set the cups down and grinned at Kristy. To think: if he hadn't started investigating the death at the senior home, he'd never have met her.

She took a sip of her drink. "Mmm, cinnamon."

"I thought you might like it," he said. Although she was usually more of a coffee drinker.

"Ah, a cozy night in."

And that's when the doorbell rang. Winston scowled. He hated solicitors. "Ignore it."

She shrugged. "Okay. For the game, I think I'll be an elf."

Somebody knocked with loud raps at the door. Over and over again. Who would be so rude?

Then a voice traveled through the door: "Winston, open up. I know you're in there. The light's on and your Accord's in the driveway. You know, it's better to park in the garage for safety."

Winston groaned. "Marcy?" He sprang over to the door and unlocked it. Yep, there standing on the front step with luggage in tow was his older sister. "What are you doing here?"

"Can't I visit my favorite brother?" She tweaked his ear.

"Your only one," he grumbled. In a brief fantasy, Winston considered closing the door on her. But he couldn't. She was family—and, after all, she legally owned the house.

Kristy came over to the entryway, and the two women hugged each other. "Good to see you again," Kristy said. "Too bad you couldn't stay longer last time because of your job."

Marcy ambled into the living room and shrugged out of her suit jacket while glancing at the coffee table and the dice. "Ooh, D&D. Let me settle in, and then I'll be the DM."

Behind Marcy's back, Winston shook his head at Kristy, but it was too late.

"We would love that," Kristy told Marcy.

Had his sister just crashed his D&D date? And Winston hated when Marcy was Dungeon Master because his characters all inevitably died quick deaths.

Marcy tapped him on the shoulder. "Is the guest room all set up? You promised . . ." Sure enough, after she'd had to sleep on the futon during her last visit, Winston cleared out enough space in the extra room for a twin bed. There were still boxes of papers documenting his dot-com losses, gaming paraphernalia, and the extra junk he'd "tidied up" from the living room, but Marcy was petite. She could go around the mess.

He led her down the hall, pausing before the guest room. He didn't want to turn the handle and show her the setup. She shoved him out of the way, opened the door, and grimaced. "Isn't this a fire hazard?" Marcy asked.

Winston waved her complaint away. "So, are you here for a conference?"

She click-clacked into the bedroom with her high heels and dodged a tower of boxes, but turned around to look at him. "No."

"Oh." Typically she came for one of her fancy herbology conventions. "When do you need to go back to England?"

"I bought an open ticket."

"But why?"

"I need to unpack," Marcy said. She closed the room's door in his face, and he was left staring at the wooden barrier, worry gnawing at his chest.

# CHAPTER 2

AFTER A WEEK of trying to get his sister to open up, Winston was at his wit's end. She wouldn't talk to him—or Kristy—about her problems. Maybe it was the syndrome of being a big sis, always needing to act like the mature *jie jie*.

Marcy sometimes kept busy, but she seemed less driven than before. She did videoconference with her colleagues on occasion, but the time difference meant she had a flipped schedule.

When Winston spotted his sister lounging on the futon with a pint of Ben & Jerry's in her hand one afternoon, he knew he should step in.

"Phish Food." Marcy raised a spoon at him in greeting. "More like food for the soul."

"Maybe you'd like to take a walk," he suggested. If she'd go out the door, she'd breathe in the fresh air. Get better. Then maybe Winston could also revive his own life. Have Kristy drop by like before. Perhaps schedule another, more successful, D&D tryst.

"Nah," Marcy said. She settled into her cushion. "Look at what I'm wearing."

Sweats. Her usual around-the-clock business attire had disappeared. A sure sign of something wrong. No wonder Kristy had insisted he spend alone time with Marcy, quality family time to figure out what was going on.

"At least go and get the mail," he said.

She furrowed her brow. "Isn't it Sunday?"

"No. Saturday."

"Oh, my favorite show's on today." She picked up the remote and turned on the TV.

Who was this couch potato in front of him? What had happened to his overachieving older sis? Winston went outside to clear his head and trotted over to the unit of metal postal boxes in the middle of his residential street and retrieved the mail. Mostly, the usual spam. But also a flyer from the local neighborhood watch.

A meeting to be held in a couple of days just around the corner from his house. He'd seen that cul-de-sac before, the neighborhood watch sign a prominent orange warning to would-be villains. This gathering would be perfect for Marcy. She was forever trying to poke her nose into other people's business—or as she called it, "improve things."

He jogged back and thrust the flyer in his sister's face. "Found something perfect for you!"

She sped-read it. (No wonder she'd done so well in her English classes.) "A neighborhood meeting? I don't think so . . ."

"You'll meet new people," he said. "And *improve* the neighborhood."

"But I don't even live here. You do."

"Close enough," he said. "What was it you said the other night about safety?"

"And I was right," she said. "Your car is missing the *H*."

He spluttered. "What do you mean?"

"The emblem's missing from the back of your Honda. Didn't you notice?"

It wasn't gone a few days ago. Great, now *he* really should go. And he'd make sure to drag his sister with him. But what would get her attention?

"If this neighborhood's not safe," he said, "doesn't that affect the property value? Your real estate investment?"

She thought about it and blanched. "You're right. I need to make sure I have enough cash flow for retirement . . . and other emergencies."

"It's decided then," Winston said. He figured they'd be in and out of the meeting in ten minutes. After all, how much trouble could a friendly neighborhood meeting be?

# CHAPTER 3

MAGNOLIA LANE WAS true to its name. It featured huge trees that would boast deep green foliage and palm-sized flowers in spring, but late October didn't show off their glory. Instead, semi-bare branches pointed at the gray sky with accusing fingers. Winston looked around and soon spotted a bright-orange sign advertising the neighborhood watch group—and near it, a cluster of concerned citizens seated in a circle.

He also noticed a few empty folding chairs waiting for visitors to fill them. Winston glanced back at Marcy, who was lagging a few steps behind. She usually took the initiative with things, but she stared hard at the ground, a move Winston was familiar with, having used it in school to avoid being called on.

"Come on." Winston took his sister's hand and tugged her the short distance over to his conscientious neighbors.

There were five people already seated: three men and two women. One of the ladies popped up like a whack-a-mole to greet them.

"Hi, I'm Heather." She held out her hand with high expectations. A smile as big as her teased auburn hair spread over her face.

Marcy didn't make a move forward, but Heather gripped her hand anyway.

Winston shook Heather's hand and introduced himself as a seniors' sleuth, even mentioning his business number, 555-S-SLEUTH. He received a few curious looks from the other neighbors, but Heather soon got everyone settled.

She looked back and forth between Marcy and Winston. "It's so wonderful to have you both here. We hardly get any couples, Mr. and Mrs. Wong."

Winston's jaw dropped open. At his side, he heard Marcy let out a giggle. It was the first positive response she'd had in a week.

"Um . . ." He was about to correct Happy Heather when a strident ringing sounded in the air.

An old man, maybe about seventy, held up his brass alarm clock and stopped the noise. "Time's up. No more chitchat." He glared at Heather through his monocle. (Winston couldn't believe the old man actually owned the single lens, like a real-life Colonel Mustard from an old version of Clue.) "Sit down, Heather."

After she complied, the old man said, "Now onto business. We—"

Heather interrupted. "Bill, shouldn't we go around and introduce ourselves?" She nodded at Marcy and Winston. "We have guests."

"The schedule," Bill said, peering at the clock's face.

A slender, tall woman spoke up. "How about we go around and speak for five seconds each?" She tapped at her fitness smartwatch. "I can time us."

The man on her right made an elegant gesture with his palm in her direction. "Ladies first. Why don't you start?"

The woman looked up from her watch and addressed Marcy and Winston. "My name's Diana. I grew up in Singapore, so I know the educational system here isn't challenging enough. A proud SAHM, I homeschool my child."

The acronym wasn't the same as SAF, was it? Single Asian Female from the personal section in the papers? He must have looked quite puzzled because Diana added, "I'm a stay-at-home mom. My husband's an international businessman and often overseas."

The sleek man who'd spoken earlier ran his fingers through his gelled hair before talking. "I'm Ryan, a manager at Elite Bank."

The last of the regular attendees, a gangly young man just past his teenage years mumbled his introduction. "Zack," he said. "Solar panels."

Then Heather burbled on. "So good to know new neighbors."

Diana pursed her lips, tapping at her watch.

Heather continued, "Oops, time's ticking. I love people, though. That's why I like to organize parties." She paused and threw her hands up with a giant flourish. "I'm an event coordinator."

Bill spoke up again. "Are we done with this nonsense?"

Heather pointed at Bill. "And last but not least . . ."

"Bill," the old man said. "Genius robot inventor. And captain of this block."

Bill opened up the meeting, asking about recent happenings. Winston nudged Marcy, who proceeded to share about the theft of the *H* symbol off his Accord. It seemed no one else had experienced anything similar.

Bill told everyone to keep an eye out but shook his head, dismissing it as a prank. "Generation Z," he muttered. "Z for zeroes."

Then Bill proceeded to drone on about upcoming neighborhood happenings. Winston couldn't concentrate, and he wondered why people weren't falling asleep in their chairs. Maybe because the metal seats were too hard. Or perhaps they pretended to pay attention and instead let their minds wander. He thought back to his latest attempt to finish the level on Hill Climb Racing and wondered how he'd maneuver his jeep over rocky terrain.

All of a sudden, people seemed irate. Heather was standing up, her hands gesturing wildly. Diana looked around with wide doe eyes, saying, "But what about the kids?" Zack tried to edge back his chair until it threatened to fall into an azalea bush, while Ryan seemed engrossed in staring at his shiny nails. (Did the man actually paint them with clear gloss?)

Winston nudged his sister. "What's happening?"

Before she could answer, Bill's alarm clock rang. "Time's up," he said and marched back to his home. It was the house right behind the neighborhood watch sign, and the residence looked cobbled together. Strange devices jutted from the roof, hung from the eaves, and clung to the stucco walls.

Heather started stacking the chairs, and Winston moved to help her. Marcy even carried a few.

As the others departed, Winston heard the grumblings:

"What a jerk!"

"I was so looking forward to it."

"A shame."

Winston and Marcy arrived at Heather's home, just two doors away from Bill's patchwork dwelling. Hers was all spic-and-span, the grass clipped and the leaves raked. No dust or dirt marred the cheery home.

Winston and Marcy left the chairs on her porch, which featured a quaint mosaic bistro set.

"Thanks, Mr. and Mrs. Wong," Heather said before moving inside. Winston caught her whispered words before the door closed: "I can't believe it."

He turned to his sister. "Tell me."

Marcy shook her head. "Neighborhood drama. They'd planned this massive Halloween party on their cul-de-sac. Every detail had been settled by Heather. And then Bill vetoed it."

Winston scratched his forehead. "But Halloween's this weekend."

"Exactly the problem."

I'm not going to get involved, Winston thought. But that was before the phone call . . .

# CHAPTER 4

WINSTON'S PHONE RANG early the next morning. He knew the number. It was his friend from Green Pastures.

"Jazzman," Winston said. "How are you?"

"Good—no, better than that. Dandy. Have you heard?"

Winston wondered what his musically gifted friend was up to. Despite his arthritis, Jazzman could (he claimed) bang out a mean Chick Corea.

"I'm playing soon," the pianist said.

"Really? Where?"

"Real close to you."

There were no nightclubs to speak of near Winston's house. Oh no. Was Jazzman's mind slipping? How old was he now anyway?

"Down the street from you," Jazzman said. "Magnolia Lane."

Why did that sound familiar? "Is that the name of a new restaurant?" Winston asked.

"A cul-de-sac near you."

Oh, right. The same place as the neighborhood watch meeting. Winston hesitated. "It's not for Halloween, is it?"

"So you do know. Well, at least the word is spreading. I would've done it for free, but Heather insisted on paying me a generous—"

"Wait a minute, Jazzman. Didn't Heather tell you?"

"What? Did she change the song selection?"

"No, it's Bill."

"The captain of the block? Heard about him."

"He vetoed the party."

"But she's been planning for months," Jazzman said.

Winston could hear the hurt and anger in Jazzman's voice. No doubt the fine gentleman had started practicing from the moment he'd been contacted, ready to perform to a more captive audience than his fellow senior home residents.

"I'm sorry, Jazzman," he said. "I wish there was something I could do . . ."

"Oh, but you can."

"Huh?"

"Am I a senior?"

Was this a trick question? Did other men have hang-ups about their age, too? "Yes," Winston answered with some hesitation.

"And are you a sleuth?"

This, Winston was more sure of. He'd made a name for himself cracking cases for the older adult crowd, although he still hadn't bothered to get the proper PI license. "Of course I am."

"Great. I'm a senior, and I'm hiring you to sleuth. Isn't that what your business cards say? Seniors' Sleuth?"

Winston knew it was a rhetorical question. "What exactly do you want me to do?"

"Find out why Bill's bailing."

"I wouldn't even know where to begin," Winston said.

Jazzman sighed. "Let me play it to you straight. My arthritis is acting up more and more. I don't know how many concerts are left in my fingers."

Winston couldn't imagine Jazzman not seated at a piano. Shouldn't he at least try something? "I suppose I could take a walk down the block."

"That's the spirit. Go do your detective magic," Jazzman said. "And if he's not there, check the Tech Museum."

"Does he enjoy learning about computer history?"

"Heard he volunteers there. A lot." He sighed. "Thanks, buddy."

"Anytime, Jazzman. And you know I'll do this for you pro bono, right?"

"You and Kristy, the best friends a guy could have." Winston could almost hear the old man's smile over the phone.

\*       \*       \*

After Winston hung up with Jazzman, he took a trip to Magnolia Lane. Bill's house was dark and shuttered. Winston was afraid to step too close to make certain, though, in case some of the old man's doohickeys would set off an alarm.

He decided to drive over to the Tech Museum. Located on Market Street, the bright-orange building with its purple dome was hard to miss. It'd been years since he'd last visited, when Winston had still been enamored with the dazzle and glitter of Silicon Valley. Now, he waited until right before the closing hour, hoping to spot Bill without having to pay the requisite entry fee. Winston wondered what the captain of the block did at the museum— surely Bill, with his grumpy manner, wasn't a docent?

Ten minutes later, and Winston had his answer. He spotted Bill's bulldog face through the giant window. The old man carried a duster, and he started cleaning the great Rube Goldberg machine displayed behind the glass at the front of the building. Winston tapped on the window to get Bill's attention. Even though Bill scowled at him with recognition, he came out to speak.

"What do you want?" Bill seemed to growl out the words.

"I'm curious," Winston said. "Why did you cancel the Halloween party? Especially since it was in the final stages of planning."

"You came here and disturbed me at work for this?" For a moment, Winston thought Bill would whack him on the head with the duster's handle.

Maybe if Winston explained, Bill would be gentler with him. "I have a friend who was scheduled to perform at the event."

Bill grumbled. "That's the very problem. Who needs performers and all that fancy-schmancy? Back in my day, you just passed out candy."

"You were going to give out candy to the neighborhood kiddies?" That didn't compute in Winston's head. But maybe the gruff guy had grandchildren he secretly doted on.

"No," Bill said. "Stuff rots your teeth. But I wanted to hand mini inventor kits out."

"To make what?"

"Their own Rube Goldberg, of course. You can make one out of all sorts of materials." Bill did a little flourish with his arm over the nearby machine. He proceeded to demonstrate how the ball moved through the tracks, spinning and spiraling by different mechanisms to finish its journey.

"That is pretty neat," Winston said.

"But then Heather changed the focus," Bill said. "Made it bigger. Wanted a huge block party. The event of the year, she said. To showcase her talent."

"You were looking forward to something cozier."

"Controlled," Bill said. He smoothed out his feather duster.

"The usual trick-or-treat scene."

"No tricks," Bill said. "I hate those."

"Well, can't you make it smaller? Talk to Heather about what you want?" Winston tried flattery to get his way. He oohed and aahed at the machine on display.

"I don't know," Bill said, but then he shuddered. "Best to clamp down on her monstrous vision."

"But what about the children?" Winston gestured to a few smiley kiddos exiting the building. "Pass down your passion. To the future inventors of America."

"Tough luck," Bill said and walked back into the museum with determined steps.

# CHAPTER 5

A FEW DAYS later, Marcy collected the mail and passed on a sealed envelope to Winston. His name was written on the front in calligraphy. He almost dismissed it as junk mail, but then he noticed that the ink didn't appear computer generated. Someone had actually taken the time to spell out his name in flourishes.

Marcy peered over his shoulder. "What is it? An invitation?"

Winston pulled out a cream card with fancy black script—and also unleashed a cascade of multi-colored confetti. "At least there wasn't any glitter," he said.

"Not like you'd clean it up." She gestured at the cluttered space around them.

He'd been meaning to move all those piles of bills, receipts, and video game cheat manuals. But his sister had taken over the usual storage room.

"So what does it say?" Marcy asked.

Winston peered at the words. They seemed to swim on the paper. Soon enough, he'd need reading glasses. He pulled the paper farther from his eyes. "It's for a Halloween bash . . . on Magnolia Lane."

"The street with the neighborhood watch meeting," Marcy said. "They must have changed their minds."

Jazzman would be ecstatic. Winston mentally patted himself on the back for changing Bill's mind. "I think I'll ask Kristy to go with me," he said. She'd love to see the pianist again—and maybe spend some extra time together.

"Of course you should ask her, too," Marcy said while picking up the confetti from the carpet.

"*Too?*" He narrowed his eyes at her.

She placed her hands on her hips. "I have to go. Heather will be beside herself if your 'wife' doesn't show up."

Winston groaned. He'd have to clear that business up fast.

"Besides, it's a masquerade." She pointed at a line of small print on the invitation.

"But you don't like costumes." He remembered that Marcy loathed trick-or-treating as a kid. Well, the dressing-up part anyway. She loved being his "chaperone," and then taking a huge portion of his candy stash for managing him. Winston had always made a costume from scraps scrounged at home—his parents couldn't afford and didn't want to buy one. Once, he'd been Tin Man, using the dented rejects from his mom's leftovers at the cannery. He'd smashed them flat and painstakingly duct-taped the pieces together.

Marcy tapped a surprisingly unmanicured finger against her bottom lip. "Sometimes it's nice to change into someone else for a while."

"But you *so* love yourself." Narcissus could be his sister's middle name.

She glared at him. "Why don't you call Kristy now?" Marcy slammed the cell phone into his hand.

"I'll do one better." Winston pocketed his phone and took out the keys to his Accord.

*    *    *

Kristy's house, as always, was pristine when he entered. She had elegant nature prints on her muted ivory walls. Everything appeared neat and tidy, and he smelled a touch of lemon in the air.

"Done looking around? The apartment's the same as when you last saw it." Kristy pulled him into a warm hug.

"It's been too long." He was about to kiss her on the cheek when a giant gray fluff ball attached itself to his leg. "Hi, Blueberry." He stroked the chubby cat on the back.

Blueberry bristled. Maybe he was unsatisfied with not being greeted first. "You're looking good," Winston said to the feline, and the cat seemed to settle down.

"I've been working hard to reduce his hypertension," Kristy said, and Blueberry purred and preened.

"What brings you around?" She offered him a stool near the breakfast counter.

He sat down and waited for her to move closer to him, but she remained standing. "Um, there's this dance . . ." What, was he in high school again, asking for a prom date? For the record, no one had said yes. He'd told his parents that prom was overrated, and watched *Star Trek* reruns the whole night.

Kristy saw the invitation in his hand and took it from him. A few stray pieces of confetti floated down. "Oh, a block party. It'll be wonderful for you to know your neighbors more."

He wiped a sweaty palm against his cargo shorts. "Will you go with me?"

"I would love to . . ." Her eyes glanced over to her tidy fridge, which had two items on it. She only kept the most recent postcards and letters from her family there. "When is it exactly?"

"On Halloween."

She bit her lip. "I think that'll work."

"It's a dress-up event," he said. "We could go as a dynamic duo. Batman and Robin. Or Hans Solo and Chewbacca."

She cocked her head at him and wrinkled her nose.

"Or, maybe, Sherlock and Watson." That got a smile since they'd met during his big case at the Sweet Breeze senior home. But then it faded. Did she still miss her old workplace? Winston continued, "And Jazzman will be there—playing."

"It'll be wonderful to see him again," she said, enthused once more. For a brief moment, Winston was jealous of the old man. Hadn't the senior once described Kristy as *hotsy-totsy*? Well, she was Winston's dame, and he'd let everyone at the party know.

# CHAPTER 6

WINSTON RE-DUSTED HIS tweed jacket and straightened the brim of his deerstalker hat. He winked at himself in the mirror and popped in a pipe for a complete Sherlockian effect. There, perfect.

He could hear knocking from outside the bathroom door. "Are you done yet?" Marcy asked. "I need to add a few last-minute touches." The doorknob started turning, and Winston cursed at himself for never fixing the broken lock.

"Okay, I'm outta here." He yanked open the door and Marcy hurtled in. He swung his head back around for a second look. "Are you . . . Mystique?"

No doubt about it. His big sis had dressed up as the shape-shifting mutant from *X-Men*. Winston shielded his eyes. "Please tell me that's not body paint you're wearing."

She wagged a finger at him. "Spandex and nylon."

Still too tight. And a bright blue that almost seared his eyeballs. "Way over-the-top."

She swiped on dark-blue lipstick. "Have a little fun, why don't you? Isn't that what being single's about?"

The doorbell rang. "No," he said. "It's about finding the right person—my Watson."

Kristy stood on his threshold, looking fabulous as always. She sported the Lucy Liu variation of Watson, with a chic black cardigan draped over a silk blouse and black leggings. A sleek leather satchel hung over one arm.

Winston took her hand in his. "You look fantastic."

They started walking out together, but Marcy called after them. "Don't forget about me."

She joined them, and Kristy approved of the outfit. "Nice costume. I couldn't even recognize you."

"That's the point," Marcy said. "Time to party."

\* \* \*

They'd cleared out the cul-de-sac for the event, with no cars parked at the curbs. Also, most of the houses on Magnolia Lane were done up with Halloween décor. Bats hung from eaves, spider webs draped bushes, and jack-o-lanterns haunted porches. All except for one abode, with the bright-orange neighborhood watch sign in front of it.

Leaving the ladies to judge the best carved pumpkins, Winston walked closer to Bill's house. No lights were on. Odd-looking inventions still surrounded the house, but no tombstones or decorations had appeared since his last visit.

Winston went over to the front door. He knocked. Nothing. Then he spotted the doorbell. It looked comically like a stylized exclamation point, with a vertical rectangle for pressing and a glossy black circle underneath. He pressed it, and a chiming sounded from within, but no footsteps approached. Oh, well. Maybe Bill was already outside his house, mingling.

Winston walked back to Marcy and Kristy standing on the asphalt, and they goggled at the growing crowd. The street had been closed off with construction cones, and people seemed to pour in from adjoining sidewalks to join the fun.

A long table of refreshments took up one area of the cul-de-sac, and Winston could see Heather heading it up. In a shiny golden gown, she smiled at each newcomer and then inclined her head at them.

Winston pointed out Heather to Marcy. "Anyone else you recognize?"

"Nope," she said. "Too hard with all these costumes."

Marcy was right, but Winston had always felt ill at ease at parties full of strangers—or any kind of mixer.

Kristy grabbed his arm. "Ooh, there's someone you know."

Winston heard the melodic notes drifting his way before he saw the pianist. Jazzman had really outdone himself. He was dressed like a stage magician with an impressive top hat and a wand. And really, what he did was a sort of magic, weaving his spell on a piano. (Of course, they couldn't lug the upright from Green Pastures, so the man had to settle for a keyboard.)

After Jazzman finished playing the song ("Autumn Leaves," the sheet music read), he stretched out his hands with a grimace of pain. Winston went over and clapped his buddy on the shoulder.

"Winston," Jazzman said. "Thanks for getting this gig back for me."

Kristy raised her eyebrows at Winston, and he gave her a sheepish grin.

"Oh," Jazzman said. "I see you've brought a very fine date, the fabulous Kristy Blake."

Kristy did a mock bow. "It's Watson tonight. At your service."

"Right." Jazzman's eyes twinkled. "Elementary, my dear."

A female voice broke into their conversation. "Encore, encore."

They all turned to see voluminous yards of fabric coming their way. The billowing material might have been ridiculous on a less confident individual, but Anastasia managed to pull off the look. Her stick figure somehow didn't look silly under all those layers. Beyond the purple taffeta material engulfing her body, the old woman wore a crown.

"Acting like your namesake?" Winston asked. "The Russian princess?"

"Hardly." Anastasia swatted his words away with her bejeweled fingers. "I'm dressing up as the royal queen—a much younger version."

"For sure." Jazzman tipped his top hat at her.

Marcy introduced herself to Anastasia.

"Oh, yes," Anastasia said. "I see the family resemblance. Same chin. But you're younger, right?"

Marcy darted a glance at Winston, a smug smile on her face.

"It's my receding hairline," Winston mumbled. Kristy patted him a few times on the shoulder, and he felt a bit better.

"You two met my brother on that Sweet Breeze case, right?" Marcy asked. Anastasia and Jazzman both nodded.

"He was there through it all," Jazzman said. "From when the administrator got framed to the closing of the home."

"Even helped me move," Anastasia said. She gave Winston's hand a quick squeeze.

"And caught the real culprit," Jazzman said. "You should be proud of your little brother."

"Not too shabby, *sai lo*," Marcy said, giving Winston a little nudge in the ribs with her elbow.

Winston felt his face growing red at being called little brother in such an endearing tone. He'd never been complimented by his sister before. Finally. And it'd only taken a little over four decades.

"Guess what I heard?" Anastasia said. "It'll be a total Sweet Breeze reunion tonight."

"But no Rob, right?" Winston asked. The administrator hadn't taken great care of his residents.

"Or Carmen?" Kristy squared her hands on her hips. Could his girlfriend still be jealous of that wannabe model he'd met?

"No, silly, not them." Anastasia straightened her royal attire. "Our friend's coming."

"Pete Russell," Kristy said.

Marcy turned to Winston. "Isn't that the grumpy war vet who tried to slice your head off with playing cards?"

He had been nicked after he'd interrogated Pete at Sweet Breeze. Winston rubbed his neck at the memory. "All in the past."

Jazzman repositioned himself on his seat and stretched his fingers. "It'll be great to see Pete again. I miss the crew." He started playing a melancholy tune, and it sounded downright bluesy in his hands.

By now, the street was filled with attendees. It was hard to see past the dizzying array of costumes: peacocks strutting their stuff, wizards with cracked Harry Potter glasses, and overly made-up clowns that had frequented Winston's childhood nightmares.

A huffing alerted them to the approach of Pete. "The things I do for friends," he said, not quite under his erratic breathing.

"Darling," Anastasia said, enfolding Pete within her royal robe.

His breathing got audibly worse, and he untangled himself from her fabric net. "Anastasia, you could kill a man with your clothes."

"I've been told that before," she said.

Winston said, "Good to see you, Pete." It'd taken a long time to get on a first-name basis with the veteran, who insisted on respect.

Pete turned to Marcy. "And, beautiful young lady, who might you be?"

She introduced herself, glowing under his praise—or maybe that was just the bright blue of the Mystique skin.

Pete kissed her hand. "A pleasure."

Either Pete had really changed his personality or Marcy had managed to charm another person in her life. How'd she do that? Not only did she beat Winston at academics, but in the social arena as well.

Kristy must have felt Winston's mood shift because she said to him, "Let's dance." Then she told Jazzman to "play something nice and light."

"Guess it won't be 'Mack the Knife,'" Winston said, referring to the only song Kristy had ever learned to play. She grinned and led him to the "dance floor," a strip of concrete to the side of Jazzman's piano setup.

The tune caught Winston's ear, and he started humming along. One of his favorites. A hit from Johnny Mathis: "Chances Are." What he thought of as *their* song—she must have clued the musician in.

Winston turned to Kristy and pulled her near. Although he could only do the box step, he felt super suave as she danced with him. Her black leggings showed off her lean legs as she moved, and her long soft cardigan kept brushing against his waist. Then Kristy moved closer in, and for a few precious moments, she leaned her head against his shoulder. During that time, everything faded but her gentle breath teasing his neck and the lush, intoxicating scent of her gardenia perfume.

He knew he was having a 404 moment, everything forgotten and his mind in a daze. A new vision flashed in his head. He imagined a time when he'd dance with her again, she in a resplendent bridal gown, their matching wedding rings glinting in the soft glow of moonlight. The same sweet perfume would surround them, and he'd want to snuggle next to that floral-infused skin forever.

Then he felt a harsh bump against his back, which ruined the fantasy. He swiveled his head to find the intruder and noticed the gelled hair right away. Mr. Elegant from the neighborhood watch meeting. What was the guy's name again?

"Oops, Ryan," his date said. That's right. Winston needed a mnemonic for the man. What about Ridiculous Ryan? Or Rude Ryan? Definitely the latter.

Winston snickered, and the stately couple turned their attention toward him. Ryan's date, a gorgeous actress type wearing weighty strands of golden necklaces that could rival Anastasia's collection, exuded big bucks. No doubt Ryan's banking hands couldn't wait to manage her money.

"Don't worry about them, Lana," Ryan said to his date.

"But that Asian dwarf looks like he knows you," the actress said. What? Winston was five feet six, hardly short—and especially not for a Chinese guy. Didn't she know that?

"Don't recognize him," Ryan said with a dismissive wave.

She pouted, showing off her maraschino-red lips. "And how much time do we have to spend here?"

"Not very long. I'm just showing my face because a client asked me to come."

She fingered one of her necklaces and lowered her voice. "This neighborhood is safe, right?"

"Don't worry—I've got a tight hold of you." Ryan winked at her and spun her around. He dipped and dove and wiggled. With moves like that, no wonder he'd crashed into Winston.

Once they danced away, Winston tried to put the incident out of his mind. "Chances Are" had ended, and Kristy and his special moment had vanished. As Jazzman started playing a swingy number, Winston decided to take a break from dancing. He took Kristy over to the refreshments table to clear his head. They nibbled on steak tartare appetizers.

"Great spread," he told Heather, who pushed hors d'oeuvres his way. She saw Kristy and sniffed, giving Winston a meaningful glare. That's right. Winston was supposed to be "married" to Marcy—he'd have to clear that up soon.

"I'm the best," Heather said. She fanned her business cards on the table. *Ace Parties*, they read. Heather was listed as the CEO of the company. "Tell all your friends," she said. "Especially the rich ones."

She smoothed her golden gown and smiled at him. Heather's skin seemed to shine under the stars.

"Are you a golden girl?" Winston asked.

Her whitening-strip-induced smile faltered. "Golden Girl? Do I look that old to you?"

Kristy intervened. "Oh, I think Winston means a beauty from the golden age of Hollywood. Like Rita Hayworth."

Happy Heather overflowed again with graciousness. "Close," she said. "I've come as an Oscarette. Like the famous statue for moviemaking, but female."

Winston did not watch the Oscars. He'd never bought into the red carpet buzz.

"How creative," Kristy said.

Boring was more the adjective Winston had in his mind. But how to change the subject? He noticed kids with chocolate-smeared faces and sticky hands, but none with inventor kits. "Heather," he said, "didn't Bill say he wanted to give gadget goodies to the kiddos?"

Heather gestured with a golden-gloved hand. "Oh, they didn't fit with the theme." Winston looked around and took in the Hollywood vibe: feather boas draped the table, black-and-white clapboards described each food.

"Ooh, the appetizers have actors' names on them," Kristy said. She placed a bit of Pattinson Pate on her cracker.

"I hope Bill's not too disappointed," Winston said.

Heather straightened a Brad Bruschetta sign. "I'm sure he won't mind."

"Maybe I should check on Bill," Winston said. "What's he wearing?"

"Um, orange and black." Heather turned to another attendee. "Try some of the Shailene Spinach Tartlets. And don't forget to contact me for all your event needs." She shoved a business card at the newcomer.

Winston scanned the crowd for the captain of the block but couldn't spot the man among all the partygoers. While Jazzman played more songs (after stretching out his fingers and taking pills on the sly), Winston wandered around and looked for Bill. But then Kristy started yawning and said she had the early shift at Life Circles, so the two of them left after waving to the others.

# CHAPTER 7

IN THE MORNING, Winston smiled as he woke. He'd loved every minute of going to the party with Kristy on his arm. He was in such a good mood that he even decided to make an omelet for his big sis. He added in fresh veggies—crisp bell peppers, tangy onions, and juicy tomatoes—with a grin on his face. The clock showed seven a.m., the exact hour Marcy arose every morning. She was like his personal alarm, which had helped him from getting tardy slips at school.

Ten minutes passed with Winston still smiling. Another twenty minutes later, and he stormed over to the guest room and burst through the door.

He yanked off the blanket. "Wake up, lazy head."

She rubbed at her eyes, mascara smearing her fingertips. "What time is it?"

"It's already 7:30 a.m."

She yawned, stretching her arms high above her head. "Why are you waking me up?"

"I made you breakfast, like a good little *sai lo*." He noticed her clothes. "Are you still wearing your costume?"

"Let me get some more rest." She pulled the covers over her head.

He narrowed his eyes at her body burrowed under the comforter. "When did you come home?"

Even muffled, he heard her reply. "Late."

"What time?" He tugged at the blanket, and she pulled it back.

"You're not my keeper," she said.

"I'm supposed to watch over you."

She popped her head out from under the comforter. "As a guest?"

"Because you're my sis." Even if she was Miss Perfect and always outshone him. "Anyway, I promised Dad . . . before he had the heart attack."

She blinked at him and sat up. "I promised *Mom* I'd take care of you. She always worried about your future."

Winston gestured at the house around them. "And you *have* looked after me. So now it's my turn."

"No," Marcy said. "I'm the *jie jie*. As the older one, I need to keep everything under control."

"By staying out late? Partying?"

She glared at him. "I karaoked. And it was fun. If I had more *dam*, guts and courage, I would've gone over the top, like that woman who swept the refreshments off the table and danced on it, shimmying on an imaginary pole."

He shook his head. "Did that really happen?" Heather must have been horrified that her elegant soiree had gone up in flames.

His sister pulled the covers over her head again. "You're not the boss of me. I wanna sleep."

The business line started ringing. Winston wanted to stay to help his sister out even though he didn't quite know how. At the same time, he hoped to flee this mixed-up scene where Marcy had warped into someone different.

The ringing continued. He looked at his sister hidden under the blanket and nudged her still form with his finger. "There's an omelet with your name on it waiting for when you wake up for real."

Then he left to catch the phone's caller. He hadn't had a real case in a while, and he didn't count Jazzman's plea for help as official detective work. But the call went to voicemail. Winston retrieved the message and heard only the first part of "Hi, it's Diana" when his doorbell sounded.

He opened the door to see the woman herself staring at him, her phone pointed like a sword at his chest. Her hair seemed wild, a static electricity experiment gone wrong. She wore a light-colored Harvard University sweatshirt with a few mystery stains on it. A sour smell hit him as she moved closer, the scent of unwashed socks and desperation.

"What's wrong?" he said.

She combed her fingers through her lion's mane—unfortunately making the strands stand up even more. "Everything. The world's ending."

He looked up at the sky. No falling meteorites. Or lurking UFOs. "I don't see anything."

"It's Bill," she said.

Oh no, not him again. "Is it about the party?"

"What? No." A deep-red color crept up Diana's face. "I think Bill's missing."

Bill's house *had* seemed empty last night. "Maybe you're mistaken," Winston said. "He's a recluse."

"Bill was supposed to help my son finish his science project for the Talos competition. My boy has to win." She swatted at her stained sweatshirt. "He needs his mentor to get into Harvard."

Winston patted her shoulder. "Calm down, Diana. I'll help you find Bill."

"Oh, thank you. I phoned Bill, knocked on his door, even contacted the Tech. Finally, I had Cam climb through an open window in Bill's house—one of them doesn't latch properly. Nobody was home. I didn't know what to do, but then I remembered your number . . ." He knew he shouldn't have mentioned his business line at the meeting.

"What did the staff at the Tech Museum say?" he asked.

"Bill hasn't been in since last week."

"Really?" The old man seemed to view the museum as his second home. Winston ushered Diana over to his office (the mother-in-law suite) and jotted down some notes. He'd been wishing for a case—and now he had one.

*    *    *

How could he investigate this? Who would really know Bill's whereabouts? The man wasn't super social. Winston sighed and decided to walk Diana back home. She needed a nap—and as he breathed in the air around her—a shower.

"So you live close to Bill, right?" he said as they walked along.

She nodded, her wild hair swaying like a huge jagged palm leaf in the wind. "Two doors down. Across from Heather."

"When was the last time you saw him?"

"A few days ago, maybe. Bill keeps to himself." She dragged her feet along the sidewalk. He noticed that she wore yellow fluffy duck slippers, but he didn't mention it. "Hard to get him into a conversation. Except about science," she said.

"Right. Like that project for your son?"

A brief smile flashed across her face. "Yes, Bill was enthused about that. Cam wanted to make a robot."

"Cam? An unusual name." Winston thought about the fictional girl detective. "After those Adler books?"

"What? No. Cambridge. Where Harvard is." She tried rubbing out a dark-brown stain on her sweatshirt with her thumb.

Ah, one of those moms, Winston thought. Maybe she'd actually been born in the year of the tiger. "Makes sense," he said, trying to win back her good graces. "So what's the robot thing?"

"Very hush-hush," Diana said. "AI stuff I can't follow. But it's only half done, and the contest deadline is two weeks away. If Cam wins, it would mean a huge scholarship."

They had walked over to Diana's house by then. Hers was not as clean as Heather's perfect abode, but it seemed tidy enough. The clutter of sneakers and a skateboard on the porch seemed more functional than sloppy.

"Best of luck to Cam then," he said.

Diana inserted her key into the lock but turned back. She grabbed hold of Winston's T-shirt and pulled him close. The smell of unbrushed teeth assaulted him. "You need to find Bill. Cam must win."

Winston pried her fingers off. "I'll do my best."

Her eyes grew wild, begging him. "I'll give you a portion of his college fund if you can do it."

"Please don't," Winston said. She must be desperate if she was willing to use her kid's education money to pay for locating Bill. "Just go in your home and rest."

"Rest?" Her eyes checked her smartwatch. "I can't. Need to help Cam finish his applications before the mailman comes by. I only have fifteen minutes." She rushed inside without a backward glance.

Since he was already on Magnolia Lane, Winston wandered over to Bill's house. Again, all was dark and quiet. He knocked on the door and even tried to peer into the shuttered windows. He turned to the gate on the left side of the house, but it was locked. He'd never been good at breaking and entering, or even hacking, as some computer nerds could do. Heck, he'd even locked himself out of his own email account before because he couldn't remember his password.

Maybe he could go through the back. He tugged at the locked gate and wondered if he could shimmy through the space at the bottom of the fence. The gap was about the thickness of the side of his head. Even if he Dance-Dance-Revolutioned for weeks, he'd never slim down to fit in the small opening.

Maybe he could cross over via the neighbor's yard. The residence to the right of Bill's didn't have a locked gate. Instead, a hedge of bamboo separated the neighbors. The stalks grew past Winston's head, but maybe he could access Bill's house through them. Wasn't bamboo flexible? Couldn't it bend so he could squeeze through?

He stepped into the neighbor's yard looking for a possible opening. He had to dodge a cacti garden to do so. Whoever owned the place embraced waterwise gardening to the max. He was trying to get a better view of the bamboo growth when someone cleared his throat—from high above him.

"What exactly are you doing?" a man's voice asked.

# CHAPTER 8

WINSTON LOOKED UP and found the owner of the voice (and house) glaring at him. Zack. Mr. Eco stood on his roof and brandished a sponge at Winston.

"I didn't see you up there," Winston said.

"Nobody ever does. Great vantage point." Zack threatened Winston again with the soapy sponge. "What were you trying to do?"

Winston got a sense that Zack hadn't liked Winston's previous actions. "Um, I was just admiring your bamboo."

Zack grunted.

"I always kill mine. The kind you find in those little ceramic pots." Lucky bamboo, they were called. Unlucky when they got into Winston's hands. "The leaves always yellow on me."

Zack put the sponge away. "Well, you need to give them the right amount of water. But bamboo is hardy. And it makes an excellent wall."

"Did you and Bill agree on the natural border together?"

Zack shielded his eyes from the sun and stared at the thicket for a moment. "Eventually. Bill's old school and not very green minded. But I convinced him, especially when I gave him a discount for his solar panels." Zack pointed to the reflective rectangles on Bill's roof. "Installed those babies myself. Top of the line."

"Great work," Winston said, though he couldn't really tell the difference between solar panel types. "Say, have you seen the old man lately?"

"Nope." He scratched the back of his neck. "But I don't really keep track of him. My hours are erratic depending on when I need to make an install." Zack looked over at Winston. "You want solar power at your place?"

"Not right now, but thanks." Winston started moving away, afraid of another business pitch. "You seem busy, so I'll catch you later."

Zack picked up his sponge again. "Aw, this is easy and offers a great view. Wipe the panels once in a while, and they're as good as new again." He lifted a bucket into view. "Plus, the gray water's wonderful for plant life."

Wow, Winston bet if he peered through the sustainable wall into Zack's yard, he'd spy a huge compost bin. Winston waved goodbye, noticing a Prius parked nearby on the cul-de-sac. No doubt Mr. Eco's car.

As Winston walked back down Magnolia Lane, he noticed a mail truck coming his way. It parked nearby, and the carrier got out.

Like his own street, Magnolia Lane also held one of those shiny metallic stands with boxes for its residents. All the mail was compiled in one location. Winston went over to the mailman, who had started opening locks and stuffing envelopes in slots. The carrier's head was bopping to the beat blasting through his personal headphones as he handled the letters.

"Excuse me," Winston said. "Have you seen Bill around? Did he put his mail on hold?"

The mailman turned down the volume on his machine but shrugged when Winston repeated his question. "Don't know anyone by name." He kept putting piles of papers into the individual compartments.

Winston noticed that one of the boxes was bulging with material. When the mailman tried to overstuff it, a few envelopes fell down. The mailman cursed while Winston swooped to pick up the letters. Junk mail, but all addressed to Bill. He handed the stack back to the mailman.

All done, the mailman locked everything up and sauntered off. Winston, though, knew something was off. Bill's mailbox had been full. The old man must not have put his mail on hold, and he hadn't taken in his letters for days by the look of things. Which meant that Bill had gone off the grid—involuntarily.

# CHAPTER 9

WINSTON COULDN'T BELIEVE the old man was missing. He looked again at Bill's shuttered house. Zack, the neighbor on the right, hadn't noticed anything amiss. But what about Ryan, who lived on Bill's left? No Mercedes or whatever the slick bank manager drove could be spotted on the paved driveway, and Winston had no doubt the smooth-talker was finagling financial deals during these prime daylight hours.

It took Winston a moment to remember the introductions from the neighborhood watch meeting, but then he came up with a name: Elite Bank. A local institution, it offered great rates on loans and mailed out promotions for its checking accounts. (Winston himself had snagged a flyer before and ventured into the branch on a whim.) Winston decided he could locate Ryan and get some more spending cash at the same time.

*       *       *

Elite Bank was a nondescript bland brick building surrounded by a pockmarked asphalt parking lot. Winston pushed open one of its double doors, and the smell of mothballs hit his nose. They needed better janitors to work on the bank's interior.

He hurried over to the refreshments area (no more coffee left, but one stale cookie remained—which he swiped). A clipboard was nearby, and he signed his name on the waiting list.

He munched on the rock-hard chocolate chip cookie while he waited. Maybe if he let the crumbs soak in his saliva, it would taste better. It didn't, nor did the cookie get any softer. Before he could spit it out, a suited lady with pearls strode over.

She read his name on the clipboard and asked, "Mr. Wong, how may I help you?"

He swallowed the cookie, which scraped his throat. "I'm here to see one of your bank managers, Ryan."

"Ryan?" She fingered the white orbs of her necklace. "We don't have a manager by that name."

"I thought he worked here," Winston said, rubbing the front part of his neck in an attempt to ease his inner throat pain. "Or maybe a branch nearby?"

"We're the only one in town, I'm afraid." She pursed her lips. "Maybe you mean a teller? There's a Ryan on our team."

Winston glanced over at the helpers behind the distant counter and squinted. The third one from the left seemed tall and elegant. He moved closer. It was definitely Ryan.

Winston thanked the woman and stood in line. By letting people go ahead of him, he timed it so that he ended up with Ryan as his teller.

"Good to see you," Winston said.

Ryan fidgeted with his name badge, which clearly did not mark him as a manager. Yep, IRL, he was a plain old bank teller. "Depositing or withdrawing today?" Ryan asked.

Winston whipped out his bank card. "I need some money…and info." He slid over the piece of plastic. "Forty dollars from savings. And some 4-1-1 on Bill."

"The captain of the block?" Ryan placed the card in the machine.

"Also your next door neighbor," Winston said as he punched in his PIN.

"What do you want to know about the grumpy geezer?" Ryan asked. "And how would you like your cash?"

"Well, have you seen him lately?" Winston took back his card and slid it into his wallet. "And two twenties will be fine."

"Nope," Ryan said. "Good riddance, too. Glad he left before the party started. He would have ruined the fun with all his rules and restrictions. Or even banned it."

"Wait, you mean you saw him leave?"

Ryan shrugged. "He got into an Uber a few days before the Halloween bash."

"Remember anything about the vehicle?"

"A black sedan." Ryan counted out the cash to Winston.

Winston heard a loud cough from behind him—probably an impatient customer waiting their turn for the counter.

Ryan grabbed Winston's wrist with his manicured hand. "You know I could access your account anytime, right?" Glossy nails sparkled under the recessed lighting. "Don't breathe a word to anyone that I'm just a teller."

"Sure, man." Winston pulled his hand away from the tight grip. Thank goodness Ryan's nails had been filed and buffed. Otherwise, Winston would have deep scratch marks on his wrist.

The Uber plus the overflowing mailbox along with Bill's no-show with the science project...Something in the story wasn't computing. Why was Winston under the impression that Bill had been around, though? He thought back to the night of the party. Heather had said she'd seen Bill—but she must have been lying.

# CHAPTER 10

ONCE AGAIN WINSTON found himself back on Magnolia Lane. The light was fading from the sky and gave a golden glow to the houses. Cars lined the streets and swiveled into driveways as people returned home from work. The slant of the sun even made a tiny rainbow on the walkway up to Heather's house.

Winston rang the bell, a happy chime that could be heard through the glass-paneled front door.

When Heather opened the door, she beamed at him. "What a pleasure, Winston. I wasn't expecting company . . . but I might have a batch of homemade cookies on hand."

"Are you always this prepared?"

"Have to, in my line of work." She motioned him inside her immaculate home. Even without any advanced notice, the hardwood floors gleamed.

He followed her lead over to a polished dining table stationed beneath a huge chandelier. The immense number of crystal shards seemed to weigh down the fixture. He hoped the golden wires holding the monstrosity up would keep the gems from impaling him. Before sitting down, he pulled his chair a bit away from the table.

Heather excused herself, ran over to the kitchen, and returned with a batch of warm oatmeal raisin cookies.

Winston took one and chewed. Now this was how a cookie should taste: melting goodness with a sublime mixture of butter and intense flavor. After savoring it, he decided to ease into the questions about Bill by using a roundabout manner. "How do you think the party went?"

She grimaced. "An utter fiasco."

He thought back to what his sister had told him. "I heard about the table dancing."

"Yes, most of my business cards scattered to the ground after that hussy tossed everything off." She motioned to a nearby polished walnut bowl, where he spotted a sad pile of mutilated cards. "Of course, I didn't get any new business contacts."

"Nobody restored order?" He scrutinized Heather's face. "Not even Bill?"

"Bill? No, he wasn't th—I mean, he must have gone to sleep by then."

"Really? I don't think I saw him at all that night."

Heather massaged her temples. "Things got worse. Somebody set off Bill's motion detector, and the floodlights lit up the place like search beams. People even started dancing in those 'spotlights'—and your wife started the karaoke craze."

"My wife?" Winston choked on a bit of cookie. He remembered his vision of Kristy in a bridal gown . . . but they'd left before that point. Had she circled back?

"You know, she was dressed like Mystique." Heather tsk-tsked. "Tight blue spandex, revealing way too much."

Winston groaned. "Marcy's not my wife—"

"I bet that's what you told your lady friend," Heather said. She snatched away the plate of cookies. "The one dressed like Watson."

Winston held his palms up. "This is all a misunderstanding. Marcy's my sister—"

"She's your sister, too? Aren't there laws against that? I think you'd better leave." Heather pointed to the exit.

"I'll explain it to you later." He grabbed one of her business cards before shuffling over to the door. Maybe he could email her after she calmed down.

It wasn't until he got home that Winston realized his folly. Heather hadn't actually answered any questions about Bill. By acting upset, she'd created a diversion.

# CHAPTER 11

THAT NIGHT, OVER their Cup Noodles, Winston told Marcy about his encounter with Heather. "Can you believe it? I said you're my sister, and she still thought we were married."

Marcy twirled her chopsticks in the broth. "At least she thinks I'm a catch."

"Or maybe I'm the catch." Winston slurped his noodles while Marcy frowned at him. "Or not."

To lighten her somber mood, he decided to keep Marcy's mind busy and get her opinion about the case. Besides, she didn't seem too busy, between the prancing around like a superhero and the sleeping in. He wondered out loud who could have kidnapped—or man-napped—Bill.

"How do you know he was taken?" Marcy asked.

Winston drained the last drops of the salty soup. "Didn't put his mail on hold."

"Couldn't he have just wanted to get away?"

Winston thought about Bill, with his brass alarm at the meeting, and shook his head. "I don't think he's that type. Seems to need everything planned in advance."

She sighed and dumped her empty carton in the trash. "People surprise you," she said, and then left for bed. How could she sleep so much? Surely any jet lag would be over by now.

Winston didn't know what to make of Bill's situation. Was Marcy right? Could it have been some sort of spontaneous vacation? His mind kept going over the neighbors' comments, but he couldn't make sense of anything. He tossed and turned throughout the night.

\*     \*     \*

The phone woke Winston up in the morning. He felt exhausted and wanted to pull the sheets over his head. Like sister, like brother.

Someone was calling his business line: 555-S-SLEUTH. He cleared his throat several times before answering—best to sound like he was an early riser. "Winston Wong, Seniors' Sleuth, at your service."

A female voice said, "It's Diana."

"Oh yes, about the case—"

"He's here," she said.

"Who?"

"Bill. Came back this morning and called me." She breathed a sigh of relief. "Apologized for being gone and everything."

"He returned?" His mind was still waking up. Winston had been sure he'd had a solid case on his hands.

"Yes. Didn't I say so? Anyway, the science project is back on track."

"Great," Winston said. "By the way, did Bill say where he went?"

"Who cares? Just wanted to tell you the good news." She cleared her throat. "There's no charge for the consultation, right?"

Winston thought about the questioning he'd done at the cul-de-sac. He'd used his time, but he'd enjoyed getting back into real detective mode. His usual senior cases involved finding lost pets, but they weren't exactly exciting sleuthing material. And, though he made enough money with his YouTube gaming channel, he didn't love it as much as solving mysteries. "Free for you," he said.

Diana thanked him and hung up. He stared at his phone and wondered why Bill had gone off. Was it so simple as getting away, like his sister had said? He put his flip-flops on and walked out the door.

*     *     *

Bill's house looked as deserted as before. Winston stood on the threshold, ready to press the exclamation-mark shaped bell, when the door swung open.

"Winston," Bill said. "Why are you lurking about?"

"Um, good to see you, too." Was he going to get kicked out right on Bill's doorstep? He craned his neck to look over Bill's shoulder. Maybe he could get a quick peek at the interior.

"Stop gawking," Bill said. "You can come in."

Winston stepped inside and noticed boxes everywhere. Carton stacks formed cardboard towers around the space. Thank goodness there was a slight breeze flowing from one of the windows. It was an old shutter that didn't completely close. The flow of air helped ward off his sudden sense of claustrophobia. "Bill, did you move here recently?"

"No. Been here twenty years—why?"

"You're still unpacking?" Winston asked.

"Oh, these boxes? Parts for inventions," Bill said. He pointed at a label on one carton. "Everything's sorted."

*Nuts and bolts*, the sticker read. It was one of those old ribbon tapes with raised lettering that shot out of a label gun.

"You sure have everything an inventor might need. Too bad the kids didn't get your gadget kits for Halloween . . ."

"Well, there's always next year."

Was the old man being evasive on purpose? Couldn't he tell Winston where he'd been? Winston looked around for a place to sit, but there was only a narrow pathway between the boxes.

And he couldn't perch on any of the cardboard towers. "Where did you go?" Winston asked. "Everyone was worried." Well, at least Diana had been frantic about the absence.

"Didn't Heather tell you?"

"She didn't say anything."

Bill shrugged.

"And you didn't put your mail on hold."

Bill narrowed his eyes at Winston. "How would you know? Snooping on me?"

"I, er, happened to run into the mailman."

"Probably complained to you," Bill said. "Whippersnappers, no patience these days."

"Speaking of patience, Diana was dying to talk with you."

"Yeah, the robot project with Cam. Want to see it?" Bill's eyes lit up, and he seemed to quiver with anticipation.

"I'd love to," Winston said. "Hope the boy wins the scholarship."

"With my help?" Bill puffed out his chest. "He can't lose."

Bill led Winston through the maze of boxes and into the kitchen. A thick layer of dust covered the countertop, and the stove seemed like it hadn't been used in a long time. But Bill pulled open the oven door with a flourish.

Winston craned his neck to look into the dark recesses. "Is your invention in there?"

Bill reached in and pulled out a robot. Not quite a full-sized mechanical butler, it stood a mere foot high. It had a friendly square robot face with round eyes and a triangle nose. Two wire antennae stuck out of its head. The rest of the body was rectangular with attached hands that had flexible digits. It lacked legs and operated instead on a roller chain, like a mini tank.

"Did it shrink?" Winston asked.

"No, he's compact." Bill cradled the metallic guy in his arms. "Meant to fit in small spaces, like ovens. But he can extend in height."

Anyway, who was Winston to judge? His own family had stored pots, pans, and even plates on the oven racks when they ran out of cabinet space.

"Besides," Bill said, "Adom's fireproof."

"Adam? Like in the garden of paradise?"

"Adom. Adam was the first man; Adom is the first robot."

Winston hemmed and hawed. "There have been robots made before."

"Not like mine," Bill said. "He's small, so he can fit in the oven. Great for baking."

So the robot was like a glorified kitchen gadget with mobility.

"And watch this"—Bill winked at Winston and proceeded to demonstrate—"he responds to voice commands, not a remote."

Bill picked up the tiny robot and looked it in the eyes. "Adom," he said, and it turned on. Nice mod.

Bill set it down and issued a few orders: "Retrieve onion. Put on counter."

The robot proceeded to go to the refrigerator. Its body then extended up like a ladder to take it to the proper height to open the fridge door. It rummaged through the produce bin, plucked out a yellow onion, and placed it on the kitchen counter.

Bill continued, "Chop onion."

The robot retracted its arm. A clink sounded, and a new metallic limb appeared, a knife blade attached to one end. Adom started dicing away at the vegetable on the dusty counter.

Tears of irritation sprang to Winston's eyes. "Impressive," he said, rubbing his face.

"Adom's a whiz in the kitchen. What everyone—single or not—needs. Now, for the last task: making juice."

Bill focused on the robot again. "Retrieve orange. Get glass. Make juice."

The robot switched arms back to normal mode. Then it took an orange from the fridge and a glass from a cupboard. After placing the fruit on the counter, it peeled the orange and started squeezing, harder and harder, over the glass. Juice started spraying out—but then Adom froze. The robot started sparking and making fizzing noises. Its extended body crumpled, and it shrank.

"Oh no." Bill grimaced. "Can't believe this is happening again."

Adom's arms started jerking, and it began spinning in circles. Then it zoomed out of the kitchen. Winston heard a loud crash from the hallway. He and Bill rushed out to find boxes tumbled all over the floor, and the robot lying on its back, its power shut down.

Winston helped Bill clean up the mess, sorting through materials and putting them in the appropriate containers. "So the robot's not quite ready, huh?"

"Almost there," Bill said. "A mere hiccup." He stacked a few boxes into a high tower.

He wanted to encourage the old man. "Right, the robot's a surefire winner."

"The next Adom, number fifty, will be perfect," Bill said. "I'll work all night long to finish it. Then tomorrow will really be a special day for me."

Wow. Winston couldn't imagine trying the same thing over and over again, fifty times. Both Bill, and Cam—Diana's kid— must have a lot of patience.

They returned to the kitchen to tidy up there as well. Bill put away the glass cup and wiped down the counter. Winston didn't see anything else to clean except for the bashed orange, which he threw in the trash.

He held his nose. "I think you need to take out the garbage."

"That's not from the trash," Bill said. He jerked his thumb toward the kitchen window.

Winston saw a streak of black-and-white fur through the glass pane. "Is that a skunk?" But the rotten smell had already confirmed his sighting.

"Mr. Nature Lover, my neighbor, doesn't want to get rid of them. Says there's a *family* of skunks. First, soapy water leaks through that flimsy bamboo wall of his, and now this."

Winston wasn't the only one to give the neighbor a nickname then. Mr. Eco was a bit over-the-top with his nature-hugging ways.

Bill shook his head. "I've had enough. I'm going to call Animal Control to round the pests up."

"Good luck," Winston said as he bid Bill goodbye. He really hoped the inventor would win this fight. For sure, he didn't want the skunks heading *his* way. It wasn't until Winston had left that he realized Bill had never said why he'd gone away for Halloween.

# CHAPTER 12

WINSTON WONDERED IF he should go back inside and question Bill some more. Before he could figure out what to do, he noticed a black sedan pulling up to the curb near him. With an Uber logo.

The driver, a twentysomething with pimples all over his face, got out and walked up Heather's driveway.

Winston hurried over and blocked the path to the front door. "Wait a minute, son."

"Who are you?" the young man asked in a small voice, taking a few steps back.

Intimidated already. The guy was just past his teens and probably in fear of authority. "I have a few questions for you." Winston flashed his official-looking business card. "It's about Bill."

"Are you with the police?" The young man started biting his lip. "I swear I didn't do anything wrong."

Winston walked over to the mosaic patio table and pulled out a chair. "Have a seat."

The youth sat down, and Winston pointed at Bill's house. "You picked him up, right?"

"My aunt asked me to." While seated, the young man started rocking back and forth.

"You mean Heather?" Winston asked, glancing at her closed front door.

The young man nodded. "I didn't hurt the old man." The youth rocked harder, almost falling off his chair.

"Where did you drive him?"

"To a nearby convention. An inventors' meet-up in San Francisco."

Winston frowned, confused. "But why?" The gesture seemed generous.

"She wanted to give him a gift. An early birthday present."

"She paid for the convention?"

"The motel. Maxed out her card for it, too." The nephew picked at one of his zits. "The admission was covered by her company."

Winston scratched his head and remembered the name on the business cards. "Ace Parties?"

"No, her previous one. Aunt Heather's flying solo now."

"She decided to move up?" The title of *CEO* had been printed on the new cards.

The nephew lowered his voice. "Um, she actually got canned a few months back. Not enough business. But she cashed in her sick days and vacation time. Plus, she got free tix to that inventors' thing."

"You've been real helpful—" And that's when Heather opened her door.

"Who's out there?" she asked. She wore a flour-covered apron, and a few white specks dotted her cheek. "Evan? Winston?" She looked back and forth between the two of them. "You know each other?"

"Just met," Winston said. "I was visiting Bill when I ran into your nephew."

"Oh, Bill." Heather patted her hair and managed to get flour on it, too. "I'm going to make him something special on account of his birthday tomorrow. Evan here"—she looked at her nephew—"said he'd taste some of my creations."

"Auntie bakes the best stuff," Evan said, his stomach emitting rumbles. He headed for the open doorway, giving Winston a wave.

"You can try some tomorrow," Heather said. "At the meeting. Neighborhood watch at six in the evening, remember?"

No, he didn't, but Heather kept staring at him.

"You are coming, right?"

Winston thought about it. He really wanted to know what was going on, why Bill and Heather seemed so tight-lipped. He felt compelled to uncover the truth. "Of course," he said. "Wouldn't miss it for the world."

# CHAPTER 13

WINSTON TRIED TO convince Marcy to go to the meeting, but she refused. "I can't show my face there," she said, blushing. "Not after my crazy dancing and screeching out 'I Will Survive' at the top of my lungs."

Marcy wouldn't budge. After the failed coaxing, Winston made his way over ten minutes late. But that was okay. Why, it was practically early according to *Asian* time.

However, everyone else had already sung "Happy Birthday" to Bill, and Heather was passing out pieces of marble cake. The scent of fudge frosting made Winston's mouth water. He took a slice and settled into a folding chair.

Everybody nibbled on the cake (except Winston, who was gobbling his), and the birthday boy led the meeting.

"Seventy-three today and still in shipshape," Bill said. He proceeded to go through a few announcements while Winston savored the comforting sweetness of vanilla coupled with the richness of chocolate.

Bill concluded the updates and said, "Now let's review our last major event, the Halloween party—that I didn't authorize." He stared down Heather, who offered him another piece of cake. Bill shook his head, but Winston thought the old man's gaze softened.

Ryan spoke up. "Expensive event." He patted his hair although it was gelled down—the strands seemed to almost sparkle in the setting sun. "I mean, so elegant. Loved the Hollywood glam."

Heather offered the bank teller a tentative smile. "I tried my best."

Diana jumped in. "Too many people. My husband and son took one look at the scene and left to go find a quieter street."

"There was a big hubbub," Zack said. "I saw someone dancing on the refreshments table—"

"Teenagers"—Diana shook her head—"I bet one of them took my wristlet."

"You lost your purse?" Heather's forehead crinkled with worry.

"It must have fallen somewhere," Diana said. "With all that hustle and bustle."

"I didn't notice a handbag. And I cleaned it all up," Heather said.

"Maybe not everything. Saw a few raccoons walking around that night," Zack said with a big grin on his face.

Bill groaned. "Great, skunks *and* raccoons."

"They have every right to this land," Zack said.

Diana waved her hand around. "But back to more pressing issues."

"How are you managing without your stuff?" Winston asked Diana. He wondered why she hadn't mentioned the loss to him before; she had only seemed fixated on her son's science project.

"I'm doing okay," Diana said. "Been getting groceries online, since I don't have my license on me. Also had to notify the credit card companies. In fact, someone's already used my Visa at Tiffany's. The nerve!"

Heather placed a hand on Diana's arm. "I'm so sorry. Why didn't you tell me earlier?"

Diana gave a little frown. "I didn't want to add to your stress. You already had the ruined business cards to deal with—"

Heather's face crumpled, and she looked about to cry. "I know—my event of the year was an absolute failure."

Winston wanted to reach out to her, but he was not very good with crying women. He'd never known what to do when his mother or sister had shed tears. So instead of giving any comfort, he pushed the cake crumbs around his plate with a fork.

Bill cleared his throat, and everyone's attention focused on the old man. "Don't worry, Diana. I'll figure out who took your purse."

Wait a minute. That was Winston's job. Why was nobody asking the detective here to help?

Everyone's eyes seemed focused on Bill, and Diana's eyes widened as she asked him, "But how?"

Bill tapped his noggin. "I have my ways. After all, as captain of the block, I have to keep an eye on the neighborhood." With that statement, he adjourned the meeting.

Winston wondered what the old man had up his sleeve. Maybe he and Bill could have a standoff and see who solved the crime faster. Despite the friendly competition, Winston was glad that the old man had turned up safe and sound.

# CHAPTER 14

WINSTON CALLED UP Kristy to tell her he had some good news, but he didn't want to spill the beans over the phone. She'd been busy at work, and he'd been sleuthing, so they hadn't been able to connect in person as much as he'd wanted. Plus, there was the issue of his sister, an unwanted third wheel. Thankfully, Marcy had planned a breakfast with an old friend of hers for the next day, so Winston's morning would be clear.

"How about we meet at the Jukebox Café?" he asked. The diner was a fave of theirs, even with its sticky vinyl booths.

"Or I could come over," she said.

How cozy. "Even better."

She hesitated. "I'll be bringing a surprise."

They weren't the kind of lovey-dovey couple who'd celebrate one month, two months, three months of dating, and so on. He wondered why she'd get him a present. It wasn't his birthday. But maybe for Pi Day, the 314th day of the year? "That's fine by me."

"You took a while to respond," she said. "How about I make you a personalized breakfast burrito?"

His stomach roared in agreement. He'd never say no to a good meal. And Kristy managed to make the most scrumptious things; even a fried egg in her hands tasted like a culinary masterpiece.

*     *     *

Although she showed up bright and early at an unusual wake time for him, Winston was ready. He'd managed to change out of his pj's, wash his face, and even spritz on some Macho aftershave.

Kristy carried in a bag of groceries. Winston had started pulling ingredients out (eggs, tortillas, potatoes) when she held up a hand. "Wait a minute. I need to get something else."

Winston was busy admiring the four-cheese shreds when she came back with a bag of cat food, a litter box with accoutrements, and a howling Blueberry.

"You brought your cat?"

"Surprise," she said.

How romantic could this date be if that feisty feline was around?

As if on cue, Blueberry hissed at Winston. Then the cat started exploring the house. Winston swore the cat's nose went up in the air while it surveyed the bachelor pad. "I don't think he likes it here."

"Give Blueberry some time," Kristy said. "He'll get used to your place."

She started cracking some eggs into a skillet on the stove. Before he knew it, she'd cooked up a mouthwatering display of ingredients for a make-your-own breakfast burrito.

He put sausage, bell peppers, onions, cheese, and potatoes into a tortilla, with a dollop of sour cream and a splash of salsa, and rolled it up. Chewing the burrito, he felt like his taste buds had taken flight. He couldn't—didn't want to, really—speak as he chowed down.

"Glad you're enjoying your food," Kristy said with a smile. "Since your mouth is full, I'll talk." But first she put fixings (black beans, cheese, eggs) in her own tortilla. She rolled it up and sat staring at the burrito. "I got a letter from Abel."

Her brother. The one who lived in Oregon. Married, without kids. A childless couple who hiked in the lush surrounding greenness whenever they could. Winston swallowed a mouthful of his breakfast goodness. "He and his wife—are they all right?"

"More than fine, they're great." She dabbed at her eyes with a napkin. "Actually, they're expecting."

"That's wonderful." Winston had never thought of himself as father material, but he liked seeing it in others. Especially Abel and his wife, who'd tried so hard for years and then had given up hope. "When's the baby due?"

"Next week," Kristy said.

"All this time you didn't tell me your sister-in-law was pregnant?"

"Well, I thought you might not want to think about it."

Winston hated talking about kids.

Kristy continued, "Abel wants me to be there since Mom and Dad aren't around . . ."

She couldn't finish her sentence, and he knew why. Even after all these years, Kristy could still get choked up about her parents.

He gave her a gentle squeeze on the shoulder. She had been like a mother figure to her younger brothers when their parents had died in a tragic car accident. "Go, then," he said.

"I am," Kristy replied. "Tomorrow. I've got an afternoon flight booked. Except"—she nodded her head at Blueberry—"my neighbor backed out of taking care of him at the last minute. And I can't afford to lodge him somewhere . . ."

"You want me to watch him?" Winston frowned at Blueberry. Although they'd established an awkward truce, he thought the cat hated him at times.

"Please. For me," Kristy said. "I wouldn't trust him with just anybody."

Winston knew the truth of that statement. Blueberry was her *baby*. There was that word again. Sure, Winston and Kristy had talked about the whole nine yards (marriage plus kids) at the beginning of their relationship, but he'd balked. He was already on the wrong side of forty and had proven a failure on several counts in his life. At this point, he couldn't even take care of his sis, a grown adult.

Kristy continued to stare at him.

"Okay, I'll do it," he said. He sounded grumpy even to himself, so he added, "With pleasure. Oh, and congrats to your brother and sister-in-law."

She beamed at him. "This means a lot to me." She took his hand in hers. "I know it's hectic for you right now. With that new case open and—"

"Actually, Bill turned up. Went to some inventors' conference."

"Wow, great sleuthing."

He didn't correct her that the old man had returned on his own. Before she left, Kristy gave him a long hug. He wanted to imprint the touch of her arms clasping his back, the softness of her cheek against his. But he couldn't voice any of his feelings, so instead he said, "Have a safe flight."

Once the door closed, he looked around for Blueberry. Where had that cat gone? He heard a purr and saw Blueberry curled up on the best spot on the futon. The cat did a little stretch and deposited gray fur all over the black fabric.

# CHAPTER 15

WHEN MARCY NOTICED the new feline housemate roaming around the living room, she grumbled at Winston. "Don't expect me to clean up after the cat."

Winston nodded. "Blueberry's my responsibility. I promised Kristy."

His sister wrinkled her nose at the sight of the litter box and looked straight into Winston's eyes. "You must really be in love."

He didn't deny it. Deep in his heart, he knew he'd be content taking care of Blueberry the rest of his life if it meant having Kristy near him.

He studied the litter box and sniffed the air. How many times was he supposed to change the thing anyway? Did he really want to store cat excrement any longer than necessary?

He put on some disposable gloves and removed the full liner. Carrying the offending material outside, he went to the front of the house and headed toward his trash bin.

He'd just dumped the mess when he heard the high pitch of a siren. An ambulance came barreling down the street. Soon, a fire engine, lights blaring and horn honking, zoomed by as well. Both vehicles turned down Magnolia Lane.

Winston jogged over to the cul-de-sac to check what was happening. He arrived to see a body on a gurney being wheeled over to the ambulance. He tried to ask the paramedics questions, and one of them mumbled, "Toppled off a ladder."

Then they bustled away with grim looks on their faces. Glimpsing white hair and a man's build on the stretcher, Winston guessed it was Bill.

He took stock of Bill's house and noticed a ladder lying askew on the front lawn. Winston looked up at the roof, where a row of solar panels winked at him in the sunlight. Had Bill been cleaning them only a few minutes ago? Did the poor man fall? Winston shook his head at the tragedy.

He saw firemen trying to secure the area to keep people from entering. But nobody was near the house—except Diana who rushed out her front door at that exact moment, her hair in a messy ponytail and her eyes widening at the chaos before her.

"What happened?" she asked Winston.

"I think he fell—from high up." Winston pointed to the ladder.

She shielded her eyes to stare at the roofline and then down at the grass. Gasping, she said, "That's really far. Do you think he's okay?"

"I don't know." He stared after the departing ambulance.

He heard a quiet sobbing from nearby and noticed a figure seated at a bistro table a few doors down. "Heather?" he called out.

He and Diana moved into the shadow of Heather's porch, where she sat trembling on a chair. Heather's hand gripped her cell phone. She whispered, "I called as soon as I could."

"Did you see him fall?" Winston asked.

Tears sprang to Heather's eyes. "He was already on the ground when I found him," she said.

Diana went over to Heather and stood beside her. She patted Heather's shoulder. "How terrible."

Heather wiped her tears away and sniffled.

Winston closed his eyes and tried to shake off the memory. He wouldn't tell the ladies, but he was certain that Bill hadn't moved a muscle when the stretcher had been put into the ambulance.

# CHAPTER 16

SOMETHING ABOUT BILL'S demise must have shown on Winston's face because Heather's sobs started up again. "I should have called sooner," she said.

"You did the best you could," Winston said, but her crying intensified. He looked over at Diana for support.

"Well, it was an accident," Diana said. "Could have happened any time. Nobody's fault."

"And you didn't hear anything?" Winston asked Diana.

"Not a single sound. The double panes block out noise," she said, pointing to the windows on her house.

Winston wondered if any of the other neighbors were around. He glanced at Ryan's home. The banker was probably at work, but Winston thought he saw the flick of a curtain from an open upstairs window. And there was no breeze.

He also looked at Zack's house. Winston noticed a flash of color move beyond the bamboo wall in the yard. Before he had a chance to investigate, though, a cop car pulled up.

The black and white's door opened, and Gaffey stepped out. The same policeman who'd helped him with the Sweet Breeze case. But also the same guy who'd tried to steal his girl.

Winston walked over to the cop and shook the man's hand, hard. "Been a long time."

Gaffey sighed. "Why is it that you're always around when seniors get into trouble?"

Winston shrugged. "Part of my job. To make sure everything's on the up and up."

Gaffey snorted and secured the area with yellow tape. After he finished, the cop asked, "How's Kristy?"

"Fine. Actually, we're going out tonight."

Gaffey raised his eyebrows. "Really? That's not what I heard at the Life Circles senior home. Said she'd be gone on vacation." Winston had forgotten that the cop's great-aunt lived there.

The man kept talking. "She went solo? Guess she needed some time away."

Winston swallowed the lump in his throat. Maybe he should have gone with her. Cooed over the new baby, cemented the relationship between Kristy and himself.

Out of the corner of his eye, he saw Heather and Diana approaching.

Heather zeroed in on the cop, a searching look on her face. "Is Bill all right?"

"I don't know," Gaffey said. He shooed them away. "Nothing to see here, folks. Go back home."

The ladies shrank back at his commanding voice and retreated, but Winston remained.

"Are you going to open a file?" he asked Officer Gaffey.

Gaffey walked around the yard, peering into spaces and ignoring Winston's question.

Winston followed him. "Well?"

The cop swatted at Winston like he was a fly and pointed to the ladder. "Open-and-shut case. Pretty simple. Old man climbing up to the roof slips and falls."

But the ladder lay sideways on the ground, almost like it'd been knocked over. Winston frowned. "He was healthy," he said. "Volunteered at The Tech. Even traveled, going to a conference this past weekend."

"You might think you're a real detective, but maybe you'd make a better maid." Gaffey gave a pointed look at Winston's hands.

Oh crap—well, he hoped he didn't actually have *that* on his gloves. He'd forgotten to dispose of them when he'd dumped the cat litter. Spotting a nearby trash can, he took the gloves off and tossed them in.

Gaffey smirked. "Like I was saying, accidents happen. And that's what clearly occurred here."

What a scrub. And not just because of his rude comments. The policeman wouldn't even think about alternate scenarios.

Although Winston nodded, he didn't agree with the cop. First, there was the position of the ladder. And, though he hadn't noticed it at first, the grass seemed flattened in an odd patch. And not where the body would have fallen based on the angle of the ladder, but farther away.

Had someone else been nearby when Bill had fallen? He tried to bring up his suspicion to Officer Gaffey, but the policeman brushed him off. It seemed that Winston would have to take matters into his own hands.

# CHAPTER 17

WINSTON RETURNED TO an empty house and sat fuming in the living room. The neighbors seemed like they'd all been home and might make good witnesses. He knew he needed to question them about Bill, but how?

At that moment, Marcy strolled in. She smelled like hairspray, and her nails gleamed with a bright-orange polish.

"You went to the salon? Do you know what you missed?" Winston shivered. "An ambulance came for Bill."

Marcy thrust a flyer into his hand. "That explains what I found posted in the mail area."

The paper urged for a neighborhood watch meeting to be held tomorrow night. Besides the regulars, though, who would be able to make it on such short notice?

"I bet it's to elect a new captain." Marcy lowered her eyes. "So sad about Bill."

"A real shame." But the meeting offered the perfect opportunity to discover what had really happened. It'd be his chance to talk to the others, to find out whether they'd seen anything suspicious when Bill had fallen from his ladder.

Blueberry came by and rubbed his body against Winston's legs. In that moment, Winston felt a twinge of misery. He scooped up the cat and cuddled it, but Blueberry was a sorry substitute for his owner and soon jumped out of Winston's arms. Awash with loneliness, Winston dialed Kristy's number. She picked up on the first ring.

"I miss you," he said before she could even speak.

"Oh, Winston," Kristy said. "I wish you could be here. The baby came early. Listen to this—"

A gurgling came down the line. Was that the cooing of a baby? He thought that all infants did was cry and make dirty diapers. Perhaps they weren't so bad after all?

Kristy came back on the phone. "He's a cutie. I could hold him twenty-four seven." Her voice had softened, and Winston could imagine her maternal tenderness whenever she held the baby.

"He seems sweet," Winston said, "babbling and all."

"I wish you could see his sweet smile."

I wish I could see your smile, he thought, but didn't say. "When are you coming back?"

"Next week," she said. "Anything interesting going on?"

He didn't want to alarm her about Bill's tragedy, but he had to say something. "Bill fell, and I'm investigating it."

"Oh no. Will he be okay?"

"I'm not sure." He couldn't tell her that he'd seen a very still body being pulled away from the house.

"Hope he recovers soon." She paused and then fumbled for words. "Did you say you're *investigating* it?"

"Yes, it's a little odd. Wish I could get your take on things." Kristy was invaluable when he got stumped. She helped him see things from a new perspective.

"What about Marcy? She could help you."

His sister? That's why they usually lived an ocean apart. Distance improved their relationship. "Well . . ."

"Is she too busy?"

Winston looked over at his sister's coiffed hair and polished nails. "Not exactly."

"More importantly, is she happy?"

Winston saw Marcy reach for the remote and start flipping through the channels, a bored expression on her face. "Nope," he said.

"Lean on each other then," Kristy said.

The baby started making a fuss in the background, and Kristy had to hang up. But before she did, Kristy extracted a promise from Winston that he'd include his sister in the new investigation.

Thinking about this agreement, Winston strode over to his sister. "Turn off the TV and listen to me."

Marcy gave him a blank look.

"We're going to that meeting," he said.

"Not those people again . . ."

"Are you still worried about your *American Idol* tryout?"

She turned up the volume on the television.

"Marcy, it's important." He grabbed the remote and shut off the TV. "There may have been a murder."

She shuddered. "Okay, I promise to go with you tomorrow."

# CHAPTER 18

AT THE EMERGENCY meeting, chairs were set up in a circle on Bill's yellowing lawn. The neighbors sat silent, avoiding eye contact. As Winston and Marcy took their seats, he thought the residents all looked worse for the wear.

Heather, although not currently crying, had her hands folded on her lap, and her face was drained of color. Diana had pulled her hair back into a tight ponytail, and her face seemed triple washed, with spots of pink where she'd scrubbed too hard. Zack hunched over in his chair, a baseball cap pulled low over his eyes, his face hidden in its shadow. Even Ryan, with his neatly manicured nails, appeared stricken. Though he had a smile pasted on, Ryan's eyes seemed glazed and unseeing.

Every one of them looked around, waiting for someone to start. Then they all talked at once:

"Who called for this meeting?"

"Didn't you see the flyer?"

"*I* didn't post it up."

Finally, Heather clapped her hands and spoke. "Seems like somebody has to lead, so I'll get us started."

Zack straightened up in his seat. "Who said you were in charge?"

"I'm an event coordinator," Heather said. "I organize. That's what I do."

"Not anymore." Ryan's fake smile disappeared. "You got laid off, remember?"

Heather scowled at him, while Diana pulled at her ponytail a few times before talking. "I'm the most qualified for block captain. After all, I'm already president of the local homeschooling club."

"Please," Heather said. "You don't get to elect yourself. In the bylaws, it states that we have to vote the person in."

As they glared at one another, a car zoomed down the cul-de-sac and parked. Winston spotted a stranger exit the black sports car and head towards them with a leather briefcase. With a balding head and a slight paunch, the man didn't seem intimidating until he said, "I'm Bill's estate lawyer."

What now, Winston thought, as he eyed the attorney in his dark charcoal suit.

"I was informed about Bill's death yesterday afternoon."

Winston shuddered. He hadn't wanted to be right. From around Winston, a mix of gasps and sobs filled the air.

The lawyer cleared his throat. "Settle down, so we can get to business." He waited for complete quiet before speaking again. "Bill wanted to give half of his assets to support the Tech."

Zack grumbled. "Of course, he did. What about all the animals in need?"

The lawyer continued as though he hadn't been interrupted. "And as he already mentioned to you, the other half of Bill's life savings he left to the new block captain, which is why I set up this meeting."

Surprised looks arose on their faces. Winston heard a mass of excited whispers and could only pick up snippets of words:

"Really?"

"Can't believe it."

"Thought he was joking."

The lawyer held his hands up. "I'll wait here while you decide. Then I'll give the proper paperwork to the heir."

"Let's vote on it," Ryan said. "Who thinks I should lead?" Ryan raised his own hand.

In fact, everyone nominated and voted for themselves.

And why not? Bill must have accumulated a lifetime of savings. An epic inheritance. Besides, who wouldn't want free money? Every one of them could use the extra cash: Heather to kick-start her business, Diana to cover college expenses for her kid, Ryan to move up the social ladder, and Zack to donate to animal protection or other eco needs.

The attendees' voices were rising, and Winston looked to Marcy for help.

Her face turned stern. "We're all adults here. We'll do a secret ballot, fair and square."

"Great suggestion." The lawyer pulled a legal notepad and pen out of his briefcase. "Write down the name of your nominee, but you can't vote for yourself. Don't think about the money. Pick the person who'll do the best job." He tore the paper into small scraps and passed them out to Bill's neighbors.

Then the lawyer turned to Marcy and Winston, "You two get a say as well. Who represents your household?"

"Well, I own the property," Marcy said.

Winston hid a frown. Did she have to tell a stranger that? "I live there," he mumbled.

A small smile spread on Marcy's lips. "As do I . . . now."

"Fine, you win," Winston said.

"I'm joking, baby brother." Marcy pinched his cheek before turning to the lawyer. "Winston will cast the vote."

The lawyer, who'd been shaking his head at their conversation, passed out the last scrap of paper.

After Winston scribbled down his candidate, the lawyer collected all the responses. People tapped their feet and wiggled in their chairs while waiting. The lawyer read each scrap at least three times before tallying the numbers.

Then he stood before them and announced, "The new block captain is . . . Heather." He extended a hand for her to shake and congratulated her.

With the meeting adjourned, Winston tried speaking with people as they left, but everyone brushed him off. No one wanted to talk. They all trudged back home. Except for Heather, who stayed with the lawyer. In fact, they were still filling out paperwork as Winston and Marcy left Magnolia Lane.

# CHAPTER 19

WHILE WALKING HOME, Winston complained to his sister. "None of them would talk to me."

"Go figure," Marcy said. "They were all crabby they didn't get the inheritance."

"Except for Heather."

"She'll be one happy clam tomorrow."

"Yes, when everything's signed, and it all sinks in—that's when we'll strike."

"You want me to come with?" Marcy asked.

"For sure." He didn't mind his sister tagging along. After all, she'd diffused the voting situation and thought of a great solution.

"Thanks, Winston."

Back at the house, Marcy excused herself, telling him she had to prepare a good sleuthing outfit.

*  *  *

The next day, Marcy was dressed in a trench coat and jeans.

"You want to wear that?" Winston asked. "It's not even raining."

"I need to look the part."

He noticed she'd brushed her hair so that it shone, and had put on blush. Maybe detective work would lift up her spirits and bring back the old Marcy.

They marched over to Heather's house full of optimism. The woman opened the door and welcomed them in with big hugs. "It's good to see you two together, the happy couple."

Winston looked over at Marcy and frowned. "We're just brother and sister."

Marcy nodded, adding, "Only brother and sister."

"No matter, a simple misunderstanding." Heather led the way to her gleaming dining table under the huge chandelier.

Once Winston and Marcy had sat down, she placed a platter of brownies in front of them. "Second batch," she said. "I bake too much when I'm excited."

"As well you should," Marcy said. "With the new *inheritance* you gained." She rubbed her thumb against her index finger, indicating oodles of cash.

"I still can't quite believe it." Heather perched on a seat opposite them and stared off into space, a dreamy look on her face.

Winston felt Marcy kick him under the table. Ouch. That was probably his cue to move things forward. "Yeah, Bill. Who knew he was so generous?"

"Right," Heather said. "I mean, he did mention last month giving whoever succeeded him some money, but we all thought it was a joke."

Or had they? Maybe someone had been plotting a sinister end to Bill all along. "He was a nice guy," Winston said. "Too bad about his fall."

Heather shuddered. "It was horrible seeing his body twisted like that. I went closer, but couldn't bear to touch him, to feel for a pulse. I had to stare at the ground to keep from"—she rubbed at her throat—"tossing my cookies."

Yuck. Wait. Did she say *ground*? "Did you happen to look at the grass?" Winston asked. "See anything funny?"

"It was flattened in a weird spot and"—she bit her lip—"no, I only imagined that."

"Imagined what?" Winston asked, leaning forward. Did she suspect foul play like he did?

"It looked almost like mini train tracks on the grass."

"Huh. Odd." What could have made marks like those?

"Speaking of strange," Marcy said. She looked straight into Heather's eyes. "It was weird I never saw Bill at the Halloween party."

"Well, he was out of town," Heather said. She pushed the platter toward Marcy. "Brownie?"

"No, thanks," Marcy said. "Heard he left for an inventors' conference—on your dime."

"Who said that?"

Winston piped up. "Your nephew."

"Oh." Heather recovered her poise. "I had extra tickets and thought Bill would enjoy it."

"How convenient." Marcy smirked. "Bill was away while you were throwing a secret neighborhood bash."

"I had to," Heather said. Her voice rose an octave. "He never would have let it happen. It was supposed to be the party of the century—until it wasn't."

"I understand," Winston said. He grabbed a brownie and made a show of taking huge bites. Heather seemed consoled after his display of munching. "You wanted to coordinate something big, the best. To advertise your new business."

Heather nodded at him. "Yes. I would show Bill, everyone—even my ex-boss—that I could organize an extravaganza."

Marcy leaned in. "But it failed," she said. "Got too rowdy and went downhill."

"That wasn't my fault," Heather said. "Must have been a few crazy neighborhood teens." She glared at Marcy. "And you, too. Dancing like it was a rave and singing at full volume."

Marcy shrugged. "Only having fun. But back to you—after it was all over, how did you explain to Bill that you had gone against his wishes?"

Winston frowned at his sister. Why was Marcy doing the questioning? Because she wore a fancy trench coat?

Meanwhile, Heather stared down Marcy. "I knew I could unruffle Bill's feathers. Any man's in fact."

After saying that, Heather offered another brownie to Winston, which he took with delight. Marcy gave him a look and mouthed the word *Buddha* while staring at his belly. He took a bite of the fudgy brownie and licked his lips. "Win a man through his stomach."

Heather nodded. "That's right. I get along with my neighbors." She lowered her voice. "Not like Zack. Always fighting with Bill. Even the night before the ladder incident."

That sounded promising. And it was high time for Winston to take the lead in the questioning. He was the professional after all, not Marcy. "Do you know what they argued about?" Winston asked.

"Not the specifics," Heather said. "But I heard the word *kill* being tossed around."

Winston and Marcy looked at each other. For a moment, Winston wondered if Heather was trying to distract them with the new info. But his happy stomach testified of her innocence—could such a generous baker really be a murderer?

Besides, the pull of the word *kill* was too strong. It could be the solid clue they needed.

# CHAPTER 20

WINSTON CHECKED THE curbside, and sure enough, he noted a Prius parked near Zack's house. It even displayed a bumper sticker that read: *Humans are animals, but animals are more than human.* Sounded like the nature-lover's philosophy.

"Come on," Winston told Marcy. "He's gotta be home."

They walked together and rang the doorbell. After waiting a bit, Winston started pounding. "I know you're in there, Zack." He paused. "Your Prius is parked right here."

Reluctant steps sounded from behind the door, and it opened a minute later.

"Hey, Winston." Zack did a double take on seeing Marcy standing there. "Oh, hi." He ran his fingers through his unruly hair and tried to smooth his T-shirt. "I'm not really ready for company."

Winston peeked over Zack's shoulder. The place looked a mess. Containers of potted plants were scattered across the floor. An open bag of cat food lay next to Zack's feet. Nearby, a few buckets of soapy water took over the foyer.

"We just have a few questions," Winston said. "About the day Bill died."

"What?" Zack started backing away and almost knocked over a full bucket. "I wasn't even around then."

"I saw you moving behind the bamboo," Winston said.

Zack rubbed the back of his neck. "Those plants cast a lot of moving shadows from the sunlight filtering through them."

Winston frowned. "I saw your Prius parked nearby that day, too."

Zack put his hands up. "So sue me, okay? Don't I have a right to be at home?"

Marcy nodded. "Of course you do."

What was this? Good cop, bad cop? But his sister's charm seemed to help Zack relax, as the man put his hands down.

Marcy continued, "We were talking to Heather, and she said—"

Zack gave a shake of his head. "Heather and I are only *friends*. Forced to be, really. We're just neighbors."

Was the guy trying to hit on his sister? Maybe after Marcy had called Winston baby brother at the last meeting, Zack thought she was available.

Winston stepped toward Zack and flexed his muscles. Or tried to. He couldn't feel any hint of straining against his T-shirt. "Anyway," Winston said, "Heather overheard you talking to Bill the night before he died. She said you used the word *kill*."

"Kill?" Zack tried to make eye contact with Marcy. "I would never use such an ugly word."

"So what exactly did you say?" Winston asked.

"I said . . . *skill*. It takes so much skill to install solar panels." Zack grinned at Marcy.

Winston wanted to kick over the potted plant closest to him, but he refrained. Besides, he was wearing flip-flops, and he'd probably stub his toe. "Speaking of panels, what about cleaning them? Does that take mad skills? That must've been what Bill was doing right before he died."

Zack frowned a little. "Bill went up and down those rungs without a problem for years—but I guess he was getting up there in age."

"It's so sad that he fell," Marcy said. She peeked into one of Zack's soapy buckets, as though reading a vat of tea leaves. "I wonder if you saw anything odd, what with your expertise and often climbing ladders yourself." Her gaze moved up to Zack's face, searching.

Mr. Eco blushed. "In fact, I did." He nudged one of the buckets with his foot. "Noticed that Bill didn't even finish cleaning. Only scrubbed the side of one panel and left behind all these suds."

"You took his bucket?" Winston asked, shuddering. What a ninja looter. Who would take a dead guy's stuff? That must have meant he'd climbed onto Bill's roof after the old man fell, maybe even used the same fallen ladder.

"Of course I did," Zack said. "Couldn't let the beautiful gray water go to waste. Look at all these plants I can feed with it."

Winston noticed how the houseplants gleamed with health—all shiny leaves and sturdy stalks.

Zack crossed his arms while thanking Winston and Marcy for coming. He must have been offended by Winston's last remark, and Winston knew they weren't going to get any more information.

Winston scooted out the door, while Marcy lingered. She gave Zack a shy smile, and Mr. Eco ducked his head before waving goodbye.

When Marcy joined Winston on the doorstep, he asked her, "Why would an old man climb down so suddenly when he hadn't even finished cleaning?"

"Are you sure he didn't slip off the roof?"

Winston shook his head. "I don't think so. The ladder lay on the ground like it'd been knocked down. And what about that flattened grass?"

She stared over at Bill's house. "What next then?"

"We need to find more witnesses, so I guess the real question is *who next?*"

"What about Ryan?"

"My thoughts exactly," Winston said.

# CHAPTER 21

RYAN LET THEM in at the first chime of his doorbell. "Thought you'd come my way," he said. "Your job after all."

"Solving crimes?" Winston said, holding his head high.

"Sticking your nose in other people's business."

Marcy gave Winston a confused look, but he wasn't surprised at Ryan's sourpuss attitude. Winston *had* found out that the man wasn't the bank manager he claimed to be, but only a teller. And Ryan had just missed inheriting a substantial amount of money by not being voted new block captain.

Without being asked to make himself comfortable, Winston wound his way over to the leather recliner in the living room and sat down. "So, how'd you feel about Heather getting that money?"

Ryan gave an odd smile, like he'd swallowed a fly. "Good for her."

Marcy settled herself on the matching leather couch. Pushing the electronic button, she relaxed as it reclined. "High tech," she said. "Why don't you come sit and chat with us?"

Ryan shook his head and remained standing.

"It's great that Heather can invest in her new company," Marcy said, sighing a bit as she snuggled deeper in her spot.

"Yeah," Ryan mumbled. "Then she can forget us little guys."

Winston sat up. "What's that?"

"Nothing." Ryan shifted from foot to foot. "Ask your questions, then get on your way."

Winston steepled his fingers and tried to be more official-looking, like a modern-day Sherlock. But Chinese-American—and with less deductive capability. "Where exactly were you when Bill died?"

Ryan stopped fidgeting, and his voice grew hard. "At the bank. Where else?"

But Winston remembered seeing the curtains flutter at Ryan's house the day of the death. "Are you sure?" He tried to lean menacingly at Ryan, but the leather was too soft and supple. Instead, he sank even more in his seat.

"I was working hard," Ryan said. "As usual."

"Anything you can tell us about that day?" Winston asked.

"Nothing." Ryan's posture stiffened, and he turned to face the door in a not so subtle hint. "Guess I answered all your questions. Time for your little investigation to end."

While Winston wiggled out of his chair, Marcy tried pressing the button on the sofa to move the footrest back into place. No such luck. She tried pushing it manually with her hand, but as she did so, Winston saw her face scrunch up.

"What's under here?" Marcy asked. From beneath the sofa, she pulled out the object that had been blocking the reclining motion—a small glittery purse. "Whose wristlet is this?"

Why did women have so many different names for their bags? "Put it back," Winston told his sister. "Obviously, it's his girlfriend's."

Marcy looked at the label. "Your gal into fake Gucci?"

"What?" Ryan scowled. "Of course not. That purse belongs to—"

"Diana." Marcy had pulled out a driver's license and held it up.

Ryan examined his shiny fingernails. "Yeah, found it in the bushes the other day. Just haven't had a chance to give it to her."

Really? Winston couldn't tell if the man was lying. Finance folks had inscrutable faces.

Marcy kept hold of the wristlet and fixed the couch so it was back to non-reclining mode. "We'll make sure to give this back to Diana."

"Right now," Winston added.

Ryan's face looked impassive, but maybe Diana could shed insight on why Ryan had her purse. And tell them more info about the day Bill had died.

# CHAPTER 22

WINSTON AND MARCY showed up at Diana's house, where she welcomed them in, but started apologizing right away.

"Oh, so sorry. It's a mess in here." Diana started picking up—dirty socks, a discarded jersey, and a pair of cleats. She stuffed them all into the hall closet. "Why don't you sit down at the dining table?"

As they passed through the living room to reach the kitchen, Winston knew why she'd had asked them to move along. The sole couch in the area was piled with experiments. A large magnifying glass lay on top of a jumble of rocks; the mess took over one side of the couch. A chemistry kit reigned over the other half. The smell of sulfur floated in the air.

Arriving in the kitchen, he examined the dining table. The straight-back chairs looked uncomfortable, but at least they were uncluttered. He sat down on one and felt the hard wooden back push against his spine. Marcy, in another chair, gave a discreet wiggle and scooted an inch forward in her seat.

Diana also settled herself down and then noticed the tabletop. She pulled aside a stack of college brochures and applications (Winston noticed an essay titled, "My mom, my hero"). "There, now we can talk."

"Sorry to have bothered you," Winston said. "My sister and I were wondering if you heard or saw something strange the day Bill died."

Diana gripped a piece of the bright-red tablecloth near her. "Why? Did the police say something?"

"No," Winston said, "but we came from Zack's, and he said Bill still had a bucketful of suds. Meaning that Bill hadn't finished cleaning his solar panels, which was why he went on the roof in the first place. According to the paramedic at the scene, Bill definitely fell off the ladder. But if he wasn't done, why did he come down?"

Diana's fist tightened around the cloth she was holding. "Good question. I don't know. But I didn't see or hear anything. I only came out after everything happened. You saw me, remember?"

"Of course I did." Winston noticed Diana's hand relaxing. She released the tablecloth. "I saw something strange on the ground that day, though."

Diana leaned forward. "What did you see?"

"Flattened grass. Near the knocked-over ladder."

"Tracks?" she blurted out.

He spoke of the first thing that came to his mind: "You mean, like a train?" Heather had said something similar.

She squirmed in her seat. "Of course not. I meant critter tracks. Pests come around here all the time."

Ones large enough to flatten the grass? Only skunks and raccoons frequented the area. Unless it was like a Mutant Ninja Turtle. No, there must be a more reasonable explanation . . .

"I was thinking that the tracks might have been footprints," Winston said. "That someone else was around, and that's why Bill came down unexpectedly."

"Another person? But it was a fall." Diana started shivering and wrapped her arms around herself. "Sometimes that happens, right?"

"I don't know . . ."

"If you ask me"—Diana stopped trembling and clucked her tongue instead—"it was that shameful party that did him in. All the stress. The shock of the event happening when he'd already said no to that willful Heather."

Winston detected a hint of jealousy. Maybe from the money going her neighbor's way instead of into her son's tuition fund?

"Really," Diana continued, "the nerve of Heather making our neighborhood into an absolute circus—"

"Mom?" A voice called from the recesses of the house. "Can you give me a hand with this tread?"

Diana yelled back. "Not right now. We have company."

"Sorry, I didn't know."

Diana grimaced and turned toward them. "Cam hates unexpected visitors. Well, you'd better get going."

Marcy rapped her knuckles against the dining table. "Not quite yet. You were talking about the party. Well, guess what we have?" She brandished the little sequined bag.

"You found it!" Diana almost squealed with delight. "I thought I'd never see it again." She snatched it from Marcy's hand.

"Definitely yours, right?" Marcy asked.

"Of course." Diana glared at Marcy. "I'd recognize it anywhere."

"You didn't lend it to anyone at the party?"

"I would never." Diana gave Marcy an incredulous look. "It's got my credit cards, my ID——"

"Is everything still there?" Winston asked.

Diana checked the contents. "Wow, yeah. Even my credit card." She hugged the purse to her chest and glanced over at Marcy. "Where'd you find it?"

"At Ryan's," Marcy said.

"Oh, thank goodness." Diana breathed a sigh of relief. "I know it's safe with him. He's a banker."

Bank teller, Winston corrected in his head.

"And rich," Diana added. "Look at that Lexus he drives."

"But didn't you get some unauthorized credit card charge? You mentioned it at one of the meetings," Winston said.

Diana shrugged. "Maybe it was a fluke. Because nothing else has happened since then."

Cam's voice called out again. "Mom, are you done yet?"

"Of course, dear." Diana got up and showed them out the door.

Once they'd exited, Marcy turned to Winston. "You know, I remember seeing that purse."

"Really? Where?"

"At the party."

The party again. Maybe the Halloween fête had really done Bill in—or rather *someone* at the event had. After all, hadn't Marcy mentioned Bill's floodlights turning on? Had someone even back then been trying to sneak into the house to kill Bill?

# CHAPTER 23

A
S THEY WALKED back home, Winston pondered over his sister's words: that she'd seen the wristlet before. He said, "Marcy, tell me all you remember about that purse."

Marcy scrunched up her nose. "It was that mystery woman's, the one who danced on the table."

He stopped mid-stride. "The crazy lady who knocked over all the food? Ruined Heather's party?"

"The same one." Marcy nodded. "I remember because the blue wristlet matched her Smurfette costume. She was all covered with makeup, so you couldn't really see her face."

He narrowed his eyes at her. "Did you recognize her?"

"Not exactly. But she had the same build as Diana. And Diana herself said she hadn't given her purse to anyone else."

"No wonder she didn't bring it up during the watch meeting after the party. She didn't want the neighborhood to remember her causing a ruckus."

"Well, kudos to her," Marcy said as she reached the front door. "It's really freeing, dancing like that."

While his sister unlocked the door, Winston's mind drifted to dancing. He thought about Kristy and waltzing—er, shuffling—cheek-to-cheek with her. He cursed himself for not saying more to her that night, for not voicing his feelings. By the time he entered his home, he felt weighed down by the lost opportunity.

In his cloud of unhappiness, Blueberry came by and surrounded Winston, weaving in and out of his legs. Well, what did you know? Had the cat sensed Winston's mood and come to offer comfort? Unless Blueberry was just hungry.

After they squared away their meals (Blueberry ate kibble, while Winston and Marcy had Salisbury steaks), Winston excused himself to make a phone call.

When Kristy picked up, he said, "I really miss you."

"Me, too," she said. "Just to warn you, though, I can't talk long. I'm helping bathe the baby."

Winston couldn't even imagine what that would look like. He racked his brain to think of something that could connect them across the long distance. "Guess what? Blueberry's getting used to me, snuggling close."

"Of course, he's a great judge of character."

Winston swallowed the lump in his throat. "You know, I was thinking about how we danced. On Halloween. During the party. It was great . . . moving our feet together and everything." He smacked his palm against his forehead. Sometimes his words came out all wrong.

"I liked it, too," she said. "Especially since Jazzman played our song."

"'Chances Are,'" he said. She had called it *our song*. They had a special secret tune. He'd try again to tell her how he had experienced an epiphany while dancing with her, how he'd imagined wedding bells ringing.

He took a deep breath. "Kristy," he said. "When we were dancing, I knew that—"

"Oh no! The phone's slip—" A splash, and then the line died.

Frustrated, he stared down at his phone with the broken connection. But as he thought about it more, he realized his thoughts and reflections would be better said to Kristy in person.

# CHAPTER 24

IN THE MORNING, Winston still felt happy about his telephone conversation. He couldn't help but hum a few bars of "Chances Are" in merriment as he neared the breakfast table, where Marcy was nursing a cup of coffee. Jazzman had really set the mood for romance that night. He thought about the old piano player with a fond smile—and then slapped his thigh. "That's it!"

Marcy let out a small yelp. "What *are* you doing?"

"Grumpy much?" Winston asked, pouring himself a bowl of Lucky Charms. He made sure to give himself extra shamrocks. "We should talk to Jazzman."

"The pianist? Whatever for?"

"He was playing during the party—"

"And observing," Marcy said. She gulped down her coffee. "After you finish your bowl of sugar, we'll get going."

* * *

Jazzman lived in a nice senior residential home called Green Pastures. The minute they walked into the place, Marcy and Winston knew where to find the old man. A lively tune permeated the home. They followed the music to find Jazzman seated behind a piano, tickling the ivories.

"Of course," Winston mumbled to himself. As always, the gentleman had dressed up, today in a top hat and tails.

The last notes lingered in the air as Winston and Marcy approached him. A smatter of applause came from the residents seated nearby in plush armchairs. Winston even heard a wolf whistle from down the hall.

"You've got fans," Winston said to Jazzman. "Me included."

Jazzman dipped his top hat. "I aim to please. Good to see you again, Winston." He turned to Marcy and kissed her hand. "A delight."

Jazzman scooted over on the bench and motioned for Marcy to sit down, but she shook her head. She and Winston remained standing on one side of the piano bench to chat.

"We won't be long," Marcy said. "My brother has a few questions for you. About Halloween night."

"During the party," Winston added.

"A swell evening," Jazzman said. He slid his fingers over the smooth piano keys, creating a whisper of sound. "Lovely neighborhood."

"Actually, not so nice," Winston said. "One of the residents recently died over there. And I don't think it was of natural causes."

"Another murder investigation?" Jazzman's hands paused above the keys.

"Unfortunately," Winston said. "It was Bill, the captain of the neighborhood watch."

"A shame." Jazzman put his hands at his side and hung his head.

Winston could see Jazzman's face reflected in the glossy surface of the piano. The old man's eyes looked half-closed, as though deep in thought. Maybe he was remembering Joe, his friend from Sweet Breeze who'd been murdered. But Winston had solved that case and provided closure. Maybe he could do the same now. "I promise to find out what happened."

Marcy added, "My brother can do it." Her encouragement surprised Winston. How long had it been since she'd actually rooted for him instead of bailing him out? Had he actually leveled up in her eyes?

Winston gave her a head nod, and she smiled back at him.

"How can I help?" Jazzman asked. He lifted his head and stared straight at Winston.

"Bill lived in the house right behind the neighborhood watch sign," Winston said. "Do you remember when those floodlights turned on?"

"How could I forget?" Jazzman seemed to cheer up as he winked at Marcy. "There was some fabulous singing going on."

Marcy shifted her feet and looked away.

"Do you know why the lights went on?" he asked Jazzman. "Did you see anything?"

"Can't say that I did," Jazzman said after a moment's reflection.

"Oh." Winston felt his excitement deflate as though his stomach had been punched. Crit happens, as his fellow gamers would say.

He wondered if he'd catch a break, when Jazzman continued, "That's because I was focused on something else. An argument."

"Between?"

"Heather and this real suave guy." Jazzman described the man in question.

Marcy must have been thinking the same thing as Winston because they both spoke the same name: "Ryan."

"Could you hear what they were saying?" Winston asked.

"No," Jazzman said. "They were too far away. Under the awning of Bill's house, in the shadows—besides, I was still playing."

"So how did you know it was an argument?" Marcy asked.

Jazzman ran a hand through his short hair. "Looked heated," he said. "Ryan was shaking his fist at her."

Marcy gave a little gasp and braced herself against the piano frame. "Did he hit her?"

"No, it was all verbal."

"What happened afterward?" Winston asked.

Jazzman shrugged. "Don't know. The floodlights came on. And Miss Mystique over here distracted us."

Marcy ducked her head. Winston knew she would never be left alone about her grooving. "Wipe that silly smile off your face," she said to him.

Winston moved from his sister's side to get away from her angry vibe and focused on Jazzman. "Well, thanks for the info. That's interesting to hear that something was brewing between Ryan and Heather."

"Sorry I couldn't be of more help." Jazzman pressed a few piano keys, and Winston knew the gentleman was itching to play again. "You know who might be able to tell you more, though? Pete."

"Pete Russell?" Winston pictured the veteran who'd shown up at the party.

"The one and only. Grumbling about seeing somebody trespassing Bill's land, he went to chase whoever had tripped the lights."

Jazzman started playing an upbeat tune, and Winston and Marcy took their leave.

# CHAPTER 25

PETE LIVED IN VA housing, but he wasn't in his spacious bedroom. Instead, Winston and Marcy were directed by staff to find him in one of the many recreation rooms. The space they entered displayed one expansive wall with a built-in bookshelf. It held not tomes, but all kinds of board games. Pete, though, was sitting at a square table with a few of his cronies, dealing out cards.       His set was almost tattered, the color faded, and the cards worn smooth after years of playing. Winston recognized Pete's personal deck of Bicycles. Except now he didn't have to play solitaire, like he'd done at Sweet Breeze. He had found himself a group of friends, and Winston silently applauded the man for getting out of his shell.

Pete glanced up at Winston and Marcy as they came closer. "Can't deal you in," he said. "Table's full."

"No problem," Winston said. "We're not here for a game anyway. We're investigating."

"Really?" Pete raised his eyebrows at them and told his card-playing buddies to take a break. He promised to give his friends the sordid details later.

After his pals left, Pete pointed to the empty chairs. "Go ahead, sit."

They settled in, Marcy lining the cards in front of her into a neat pile.

"It's about Halloween," Winston said.

Pete tapped his bad leg. "A lot of walking that night, and a little bit of waltzing." He looked over at Marcy. "Unlike others, no extreme entertaining for me."

Marcy's hand fluttered on the table, knocking over the stack of cards near her.

"One of the residents from the neighborhood died," Winston said. "And I don't think it was an accident. It may have something to do with the floodlights coming on—"

"I remember that," Pete said while helping Marcy gather and rearrange the cards into a tidy stack.

"Did you see anything?" Winston asked. "Jazzman said you might have chased someone?"

"That pianist doesn't miss a thing." Pete tapped a card in thought. "I saw somebody dressed in black carrying something the size of a plate near the side of the house."

"The area on the left or right?" Marcy asked.

"Had bamboo on that side."

By Zack's house then, Winston thought. "Did you catch the guy?"

"No. My blasted leg," Pete said. "When I leaned against Bill's garage door to rest, I saw him squeeze past the bamboo over to the backyard . . . but then he returned moments later. I called out, but he scuttled into the house next door, so I figured he was a neighbor."

Winston groaned. "Probably Zack, checking on Bill's place."

Pete nodded. "The man didn't seem to be dangerous, so I let him be."

It was still odd behavior, though, even for Zack. "Why would he be sneaking into Bill's yard?" Not to gather more gray water.

"Well, you could always chat with Anastasia. She had her eye on all the young men at the party."

That sounded about right and it wasn't a half-bad idea.

# CHAPTER 26

WINSTON AND MARCY visited Anastasia at the Silicon Valley Skilled Nursing Facility. Confined three patients to a rectangular room, Anastasia still tried to make her separate area bright and cheery. She had even hung up a silk curtain for privacy.

Lying in her bed, swathed in her usual layers (this time, made of satin), she pointed to her "visitors' area." In the corner, Winston noticed a bright-orange fabric ottoman.

"Nesting," she told Winston, so he pulled out a mini ottoman from the larger one. His sister made him sit on the smaller version because she was a half-inch taller.

"Sorry. Don't have any refreshments, my dears." Anastasia gestured to her empty water pitcher, her bangles jangling with the movement.

"Not a problem," Winston said. "Besides, we're here for your company."

She beamed at him and extended her thin hand for him to kiss. He almost couldn't find a spot, what with all those glittering bracelets sliding down her wrist.

Marcy straightened up on the ottoman. "It's about the men at the Halloween party."

Anastasia's eyes twinkled. "Oh, lots of wonderful specimens. Which one?"

Winston described the physical features and personality of both of the male suspects, Ryan and Zack.

Anastasia turned toward Marcy. "Which one drew your attention? Mr. Fancy Pants or Earth Man?"

Marcy looked startled. "Neither"—she twiddled her fingers—"I'm taken."

Hadn't Anastasia noticed his sister's wedding band? But when Winston looked, he realized that Marcy's left ring finger was bare. Had she taken it off? Where was her usual one-carat diamond? Marcy's lips flattened into a thin line, and he knew not to ask her in front of company . . . or anytime soon.

Anastasia fluffed out her hair, drawing the attention back to her, and Winston noticed the jewels on her ring-laden fingers sparkling. "Here are my thoughts. Ryan's a polished operator. He had the clothes down, but all borrowed. Men's Wearhouse, I recognize their styles." She sniffed. "His date was the real deal—dressed to the nines in this season's fashion. But she took a break to find champagne, and he ran off to fight with the organizer girl."

"Heather?" Winston leaned forward and almost fell off his mini seat. "You saw them argue?"

"I heard Ryan say, 'Pay me back' before I got distracted by the cat burglar."

"Zack," Marcy said. She scooted her ample ottoman closer to Anastasia's bed.

"Very sleek, dressed in black. I saw him sneak into his neighbor's yard with something in his hands."

"What was it?" Winston asked.

"Hard to say, maybe something circular. It was dark, but I know he didn't have it when he returned."

"Curious," Winston said. "Did you actually talk to either of the men?"

"No, I was enjoying the party. Glorious food, great dancing partner."

"Who'd you dance with?"

"Pete, of course."

"Even with his leg?"

"Oh, he can still cut a rug." Anastasia smiled, and her eyes stared off into the distance.

Winston was glad she had fond memories of the evening. He gave her a big hug before they left.

As they walked out, Winston said to his sister, "Not everything is well on Magnolia Lane."

She made an assenting noise. "Fighting between Heather and Ryan. Zack sneaking into Bill's yard. If only we knew what really happened that night—if only I'd kept an eye on the neighborhood better."

Marcy's words rang in Winston's head, an echo of something he'd heard during a previous neighborhood watch meeting.

"I know where to go next," he said, steering the car back to the now familiar cul-de-sac.

# CHAPTER 27

WINSTON AND MARCY stood staring at Bill's house.

"Why are we here?" Marcy asked.

"Because Bill said he always kept an eye on the neighborhood—but how exactly?" Winston gestured at the doohickeys scattered around the building, the inventions hanging off the eaves.

He and Marcy looked at all the gadgets. They discovered fancy bird feeders and automatic watering systems. They uncovered a device that swept up fallen leaves into neat piles. Even a gutter sweeper numbered among Bill's mechanical creations. But nothing that *kept watch*.

Marcy placed her hand on the doorknob. "I wish we could ring this bell, and out Bill would pop. He'd be able to answer our questions." For now, she put her head in her hands. "I need some valerian."

Winston glanced at the doorbell. Its exclamation shape mocked him. This investigation was glitching, and he didn't know how to fix it.

Wait a minute. What kind of man used punctuation as a ringer? Maybe a writer. Not an inventor, though, unless he had a solid reason to do so. Winston peered at the point of the "exclamation mark" closely—it looked cracked. He then realized that the circle was actually the glass eye of a video camera—and he bet it'd been recording everything, from Halloween night until Bill's untimely death. And somebody had tried to break it, to erase the footage.

"We need to get those videos," Winston said. He pulled out his cell phone and scrolled through the contacts. Had he erased the name out of spite, or was it still there? Relief flooded him. Officer Gaffey's direct line remained on his list of keepers.

He dialed and got the policeman on the line. Gaffey didn't seem happy to hear from him. "Why are you calling me, Winston?"

Winston swore he could almost hear the man drumming his fingers against a desk. "It's about Bill's case."

"Who?"

"The old man who lived on Magnolia. Does the station have his belongings? Computer, phone?"

"Winston, this isn't CSI. That man's death was an accident. An unhappy fall down a ladder, end of story."

"So all his stuff is still inside his home?"

He groaned. "Why? You're not thinking about breaking and entering, are you?"

"Me? Of course not." Winston thanked the policeman and hung up.

Then he turned to his sister and said, "Look for an open window. When I last visited, Bill had one that didn't quite shut." He remembered feeling grateful for that slight breeze among the cramped clutter of Bill's belongings.

Besides, it wasn't breaking and entering if there was already easy access, right? Or so Winston justified to himself as he and Marcy scooted themselves through the window.

Marcy squeezed through with ease, but Winston huffed and puffed his way in. He even knocked over a few of Bill's boxes as he tumbled through the small window opening. His sister shook her head at him.

After he caught his breath, they decided to split up to search the different rooms. However, when they regrouped, neither of them had located a device. No smartphone or laptop in sight.

Winston sighed and started restacking the cartons he'd knocked over. As he did so, he noticed a boxy shape hidden in the corner with a tablecloth draped over it. He tugged the fabric off and revealed a CRT monitor. The tower featured a floppy disk drive. An actual working clunky desktop plugged into an outlet. Ah, Bill had used old-school tech. Maybe this computer had the information they needed? But why was it turned off? Wouldn't the security camera need to be connected to a running computer?

He booted it up and waited for everything to power on. After it loaded, he searched for video files on the drive. A list of them popped up, arranged by date. On further inspection, though, he noticed no videos past October 31. It seemed someone had already deleted the most recent ones.

"Come and watch," he told his sister as he cued up the video from Halloween night. They sat cross-legged on the hard floor, watching the events unfold on the screen.

They saw Heather's look of horror as chaos unfolded. A liberated Diana in a Smurfette costume danced on the table and dropped her purse in the midst of busting a move. Ryan and Heather could be seen at the far side of the screen, standing on the porch. Although their voices couldn't be heard, they seemed angry. Ryan tried to grab Heather's purse—she shook her head at him and backed away. Then the floodlights blazed on and Marcy's silhouette could be seen wiggling away as she sang with abandon.

Watching the replay, Winston saw Marcy's cheeks heat up with color, but after it ended, she stood up and gave a mock bow.

Winston gave her a thumbs-up. "You definitely have the music ability in our fam."

He played the video again and recorded it with his phone. Poor resolution, but it might do as evidence. Then Winston turned off the computer and said to Marcy, "Seems like every single one of the neighbors acted odd that night."

"Yes," Marcy said, "Did you see the heated exchange between Heather and Ryan?"

"Time to investigate more." Winston stood up and brushed off his pants. "Let's shine a light on both those suspects."

"Two for the price of one," Marcy said as they left Bill's house and headed over to the bank to catch Ryan off guard.

# CHAPTER 28

WHEN THEY ENTERED the doors of Elite Bank, Winston marched straight to the counter. However, he didn't see Ryan, so he asked a female teller for the man's whereabouts.

"Ryan?" She patted a stray lock of hair into place. "He's taking a break."

Winston thanked her and swiveled around to head over to the refreshments area, but Marcy tugged on his sleeve.

"Not over by the coffee," she said. "He's at a desk." She pointed, and Winston's gaze followed her finger.

Sure enough, Ryan was making himself comfy at a banker's desk. He removed the real owner's nameplate and squirreled it away in a drawer. Next, he focused on placing a nearby picture frame facedown on the table.

Winston and Marcy strode over to him, and Ryan startled.

"Oh, didn't expect to see you guys here." He nodded at Winston. "No lines today, you can use another teller."

"I'm not here for money," Winston said, although truth be told, he was running short on cash.

Marcy pulled out a chair near the desk and sat down with her arms crossed. "We're here to question you about the Halloween party."

Winston took a seat and waited to see Marcy work her bad cop act.

Ryan frowned. "The party feels so long ago. Well, I was dancing the night away when a buffoon"—he looked over at Winston—"knocked into me and my date."

"No, we don't need to hear about that," Winston said. "We want to know about your argument."

Marcy fixed her gaze on Ryan. "With Heather." Even Winston could feel the sting of her look. He'd experienced that same fierceness many times before, when his sister had tried to pry the truth from him. It usually worked.

"Oh, that was nothing." Ryan did a half shrug. "A squabble." He faltered under her gaze. "I didn't do anything wrong."

"Why'd you try to grab her purse then?" Winston asked.

"What makes you think that?"

"We have it on tape," Marcy said. "Everything. Recorded."

Ryan gulped. "She owed me, but it's squared away now," he said. "Honest." He crossed his heart and then his eyes darted around. "I'm actually waiting for somebody . . ."

Winston felt a shadow pass over him, and he looked up to see Lana, Ryan's date from Halloween night, dressed in an elegant blue skirt suit with crystal buttons.

Fingering an expensive-looking necklace, she said to Ryan, "Reservations at the Ritz will not wait, Honey Bunches."

Marcy noticed the new arrival and apologized for taking up their time. Leaning close to the woman, she complimented Lana on her necklace. "Very pretty."

"Thank you." Lana fidgeted with the delicate chain holding a pure gold charm. "A Tiffany from my Honey Bunches."

Looking at the joy on Lana's face, Winston wished he could make the same happiness appear in Kristy's eyes. What kind of gift could he get his girl to make *her* face shine like that?

Marcy and Winston left the bank, and he griped about their experience. "We didn't get a single thing out of him."

"Not much," agreed Marcy. "But *she* told us a lot."

"Lana did?"

"Her necklace was from Tiffany's—like that charge on Diana's card."

Winston snapped his fingers. "That's it then. Ryan did it for the money. Tried to steal Heather's purse. Took Diana's card. And pushed over Bill to get the inheritance."

Winston felt so elated over his theory that he even opened the passenger-side car door for Marcy.

"Not so fast, Sherlock," his sister said. "Ryan didn't take any of Diana's cash, remember? Left it, in fact. And I know his type. All razzle-dazzle. He doesn't need a whole lot of money, just enough to fake it."

"What about the Tiffany?"

"A chance to boost his cred with Lana. If he sinks his hooks into her, he'll have all the dough he needs in the future."

Winston scratched his chin. "But what did he want from Heather if not money?"

"That's a question we'll need to ask her." Marcy buckled her seatbelt. "On to the next stop, Sherlock."

# CHAPTER 29

THEY DROVE TO Heather's place, where they received a warm welcome and were ushered over to her kitchen table.

"It's nice to have guests," Heather said, putting a few warm cinnamon rolls out for them. (Winston snatched one up right away.) "Entertain people, instead of numbers."

"How is your new business going?" Winston asked, between bites of gooey icing.

"Getting there," Heather said.

Marcy refused a cinnamon roll and asked her, "No trouble in your life? Maybe from Ryan?"

Heather gave her a funny look. She hung her apron on the back of a chair and took a seat next to them. "My neighbor?"

Winston swallowed the last of the bun, wiped his hand across his mouth, and picked up another one before speaking. "Your argument with Ryan on Halloween—we saw it."

Heather blinked at him while Marcy explained: "Bill recorded it all."

"Secret video camera," Winston said.

Heather fiddled with the empty platter at the table. (Had he really eaten two buns? Winston's stomach emitted a giant wave of pleasure. Guess so.) "I'm not surprised Bill had some sort of surveillance," she said. She stopped moving the plate around and made eye contact. "You want to know the truth? It's simple. I borrowed from the bank. Ryan pulled some strings to make it work. Then when that dancing fiasco happened"—she shook her head remembering it—"I knew my dreams were dashed. The Halloween party was supposed to showcase my talent, bring in top-notch clients. I invited everyone I'd thrown a party for before—and their friends."

Winston nodded, following her train of thought. "After the failure, you weren't sure you could pay the loan back."

Heather wrung her hands. "I'd used up my savings, borrowed from my line of credit."

All those glamorous touches, Winston thought, bought with Heather's hard-earned money.

"We saw Ryan try to yank your purse," Marcy said.

"He wanted me to pay up, to give him something. But I had nothing."

Winston patted Heather's shoulder. "Until now. Thankfully."

She gave him a grateful look. "Bill was an angel. I don't know what I'd do without the inheritance. I paid back the loan and still have a little left over."

That must have been what Ryan meant when he said everything was squared away now. Winston wondered how the teller had secured the loan in the first place. Had it been on the up-and-up?

"Well, you can move forward now," Winston said. "What with your baked goods"—he patted his stomach—"folks will flock to your parties."

"Do you want some more?" Heather asked. "I still have a few cooling on the rack."

Winston wanted to say yes, but his sister gave him a severe side glance. "Uh, maybe next time."

Marcy and Winston both thanked Heather for her time and then left the sugar-scented house.

As they made their way back to Winston's place, Marcy said, "She still could have done it. Plotted Bill's fall, for the money."

Winston's hands gripped his steering wheel. "No, she was so distraught when the old man died."

"Could have been faking." Marcy made a few whimpering noises that might have doubled for crying.

Winston parked in his driveway. "I just can't see it."

"Maybe it's those treats talking," Marcy said, pointing at his stomach.

"No. How could she have predicted she'd inherit the money?" Winston continued, "And she called the ambulance, right?"

Marcy nodded.

"If she had murdered Bill, she wouldn't have dialed 911 right away. She'd want extra time to erase any evidence."

"Good point." Marcy unbuckled herself and went inside the house.

\*　　　\*　　　\*

Spent from the day, Winston was glad Marcy busied herself in the kitchen with dinner. If left up to him, they'd be slurping down bowls of instant ramen. Marcy, though, made a healthy vegetable stir-fry for them. She even fed Blueberry, who immediately purred at Marcy's kindness. How quick that cat changed alliances.

After dinner, Winston went straight to bed. He worried that Blueberry's transfer in devotion could somehow predict Kristy's change of heart in the future. Logically, he knew Kristy couldn't call him because her phone had fizzled in bathwater (she'd emailed him the news), but having no verbal communication with her unnerved him. He tossed and turned in bed all night. The mewling cries of some unearthly creature (Blueberry?) didn't help him sleep either.

# CHAPTER 30

WINSTON COULDN'T STOP yawning in the morning. Even the extra sugar boost from his cereal didn't keep his head from nodding. He looked over at Marcy, who seemed her usual composed self. At the kitchen table, she sipped coffee while perusing the newspaper.

"Did you sleep okay?" he asked.

"Yes. Why?"

"Blueberry kept me up all night with his yowling. Did he sneak out through the kitchen side door?"

"He's a cat, not a magician." She folded up the paper. "Besides those sounds were from wild animals."

"Or, maybe, cats mating?" Winston tried to remember if Blueberry had been neutered. He hoped so.

"I remember weird screeching, almost like fighting noises," Marcy said. She shrugged and finished her coffee. "But I just popped in my ear plugs and slept."

"You carry some around?" Please don't say it's because of my snoring, he thought.

"For the plane," she said. "To cancel out noise."

Winston rubbed at his eyes and reached for the paper. Where were the funnies? Maybe laughter would wake him up.

Marcy grimaced and pointed at the newsprint. "Yeah, all that horrible news from around the world may keep your eyes open."

Around the world—he had been meaning to broach the topic again. "Speaking of, why are you here, Marcy? So far from home?"

"Home." Marcy seemed to choke on the word. "They say family is home. And that's what you are, Winston."

"But what about Gary?"

Her hands gripped her mug tight. She could destroy it with that kind of hold. "We needed a break."

"Oh no, are you okay?" he asked, frowning. He'd heard about stress in their marriage before, over their difficulty in having kids.

Marcy's voice shook. "Guess it's time I told you. He made a Tinder account. Window-shopping he called it." Picking up her mug, she moved over to the sink and started rinsing it. "But I need distance to reevaluate."

"Either way, I'll be here for you," Winston said. The rushing water probably drowned out his words, but he'd said them out loud at least. A few moments later, though, her shoulders seemed to relax a tiny bit.

He turned his attention to the newspaper. He placed aside the various sections: National, Sports, Local—an article caught his eye. A photo of a geeky kid clutching Bill's robot took over the page.

Winston read about how Cam had won first place, securing a scholarship to the college of his choice. Judges were impressed with the robot's mechanisms, how it took voice orders, differentiating between users. And its innovative "predictive mode," where it took previous commands and tried to guess at a possible instruction based on its stored database. Kind of like the auto-complete feature on cell phones. Bill really had been pure genius.

But right now Winston couldn't take his eyes off the boy in the photo wearing huge glasses and a shy grin. Cam. He'd been around when Bill had been killed. After all, Diana had been there that day, so the boy might have witnessed something.

Winston remembered Diana saying Cam didn't enjoy visitors. Maybe not human company, but what about an animal? Winston grabbed Blueberry's leash and called Marcy over. "We're taking the cat for a stroll."

# CHAPTER 31

WINSTON HOOKED THE leash onto Blueberry. For most of the way, the cat moved at a smooth pace. When they arrived at Diana's doorstep, Winston let go of Blueberry's tether to smooth out the wrinkles in his T-shirt and make himself more presentable. He wanted Cam to see them as desirable company (cute cat plus two friendly neighbors) when Marcy's voice broke into his fantasy.

"The cat bolted!" she yelled.

Winston looked around, and sure enough, Blueberry had taken off. The leash trailed behind the cat. Blueberry made straight for Bill's house, and Winston darted after the cat.

Unfortunately, Winston had never run a five-minute mile in his life. Maybe more like a fifteen-minute mile. Marcy, the better athlete, also tried chasing, but her heeled sandals slowed her down.

Blueberry was about to spring up and over Bill's fence when Winston caught up. The cat's haunches tensed, and Winston tackled him. If only Winston's PE teacher could see him now.

They returned to Diana's house a bedraggled group. Marcy limped. Winston's arms were decorated with scratch marks. And Blueberry kept hissing like a possessed banshee. Winston rang the doorbell.

Instead of Diana opening the door, a teen boy slouched in the corner of the wooden frame. He had bowl-cut hair and huge glasses took up half his face. His skin seemed a minefield of zits, and he wore a striped shirt with polka-dot shorts. Around his neck, lay a heavy silver chain with a letter on it.

Marcy hobbled closer to the boy and extended her hand. "Cam? My brother and I live around the corner. We know your mom."

Cam looked Winston over, maybe trying to see if he was a threat. "I've seen you two before," Cam said. "At a neighborhood meeting. Looked out the window with my binoculars."

A people watcher. He'd make a great witness, Winston thought.

"So you know us then," Marcy said. "Mind if we come in?" She'd taken off her shoes at this point and seemed ready to fall into the house.

"I'm not supposed to let strangers in." He played with the metal chain around his neck. Winston could spy a pendant attached to the thick metal rope and recognized it right away.

"Nice *H* symbol," Winston said.

Cam's face grew pink. "Uh, thanks."

"Fits perfectly into that blank space on my car's trunk."

Cam backed away several inches, while Winston advanced toward him. "What other *Grand Theft Auto* pranks are you pulling?"

Cam wrung his hands. "It was just the once, I swear."

"Really? And why the *H*, not a *C* for your name?"

"For Harvard. A dare from my Academic Decathlon captain," Cam mumbled.

Winston snorted but believed the trembling teen. "Fine. How about you let us in, and I'll forget about the damage to my Accord?"

"Thanks." Cam lowered his eyes. "Just so you know, Mom's not home. She's at the store grabbing Martinelli's."

"Ah, that's right. Gratz on your big award! A scholarship and everything." He tried to give Cam a high five, but the boy didn't respond.

Winston and Marcy marched into the house, still filled with science experiments and schoolwork. Winston dragged Blueberry into the living room, where the cat rolled into his signature ball. "Like animals?" he asked Cam. "Want to pet him?"

"Nah. I don't do live things." The teen looked at Blueberry as though the cat might unleash some Pokémon power from his curled position. "But my mom might. Could make her less stressed about college apps."

Marcy shook her head. "Yeah, I remember all those crazy deadlines."

Winston had only ever applied to his local community college, and that was one application too many for him. "She helping you with the forms?"

"Kind of. Looks them over. Tells me to put down the right extracurriculars, dictates my essays," Cam said. "She even Googles my name to make sure I look good online. Says admissions might run a Web search on applicants."

Winston looked over at Marcy and raised his eyebrows. What would prospective colleges say if they saw Cam's mom dancing like a stripper?

Marcy stared with longing at the couch, which Winston noted was still overtaken by a chemistry kit. Sighing, his sister sat down on a nearby rug and rubbed her feet. She told Cam, "Don't worry. You made that great robot. You're a shoo-in."

Cam fiddled with his glasses. "Well, Mr. Bill and I did it together. He even pulled an all-nighter to create the final version."

"Bill was a genius," Winston said.

Cam started picking one of his pimples, and Winston hoped the boy wouldn't pop it in his nervousness. "He could have made even cooler stuff if . . ."

Winston looked Cam in the eyes (in fact, he and the teen were about the same height) and said, "I miss Bill, too."

Cam sniffled a little but didn't say anything more.

"Did you happen to, uh, see him fall?" Winston asked.

"No, I was organizing my rock collection." The boy seemed totally serious. "But I remember Mom running into my room, saying something bad had happened. Then she thrust the robot into my arms."

He took a wavering breath and continued, "I heard the sirens, the ambulance, but I didn't want to look. I distracted myself by fixing Adom."

"Was the robot broken?"

"Minor problem. Needed a new tread to move around. The old one got gunked up with mud and grass."

Winston had heard the boy mention *tread* before in this very same house. For the robot. To move.

The tracks, Winston thought. Flattened grass near where Bill had fallen. The robot had been at the crime scene.

"Can I look at Adom?" Winston asked.

"Sure." A genuine smile popped up on Cam's face.

Cam brought the little robot over and placed it at Winston's feet. Just when Winston was about to scoop Adom up, the door opened and in walked Diana.

She stared at them in her living room, and the bag of groceries slipped from her hands. Something shattered. Glaring at Winston and Marcy, she asked, "What are you doing in my home?"

# CHAPTER 32

DIANA STOOD LOOKING at them with her hands on her hips. She didn't glance down at the groceries on the floor, not even once. "Cam, go to your room."

After the boy left, she tried to lunge for the robot, but Blueberry hissed at her sudden movement. Diana retreated, and Marcy grabbed Adom.

"That's my property," Diana said, trying to reach Marcy, but Winston stepped between them.

"It's Bill's," he said. "You want it? Go and talk to his estate lawyer."

"Cam built it." She gazed with longing at the robot.

"It's evidence," Winston said. "In a murder case."

Diana's face drained of color. "You've no proof."

Marcy jerked her thumb in the direction Cam had gone. "Did you do it for your son? Think he'd get a guaranteed sum from Bill? After all, the old man was the kid's mentor."

"You think I killed Bill?" She looked at them with wide eyes. "I did nothing of the sort."

"The robot was there. And you have it now in your house"—he crossed his arms—"explain that."

"Yes, the robot was near Bill's place, but I found it. Afterward. Bill had already fallen down."

Was she telling the truth? Could it really be a simple case of finders keepers? Winston needed Diana to be honest, so he pulled out his ace card.

"We have a video," he said. "Of you dancing . . . like you were on a pole."

She cringed. "That can't be. I saw the broken doorbell lens."

"You mean you tried to crack the device, right?"

Her face flushed red, and Winston continued, "The footage was stored elsewhere, on a computer."

"Impossible. Bill didn't carry a smartphone or tablet…"

"It was old tech," Winston said. "A desktop."

She backed away from him. "What are you going to do with the footage?"

"Maybe post it on YouTube—tagged with your name, Cam's name, and all the colleges he's applying to."

She gasped and covered her mouth.

"Unless you cooperate. Tell us the whole truth."

She held up her hands. "Okay, I will. I *was* there that day."

"So you are the murderer." Winston wanted to drag her over to the police station right then.

"I'm not," she said. "But I did see something."

Her cheeks reddened as she continued, "I heard a strange whirring and looked out my window. I saw Adom speeding out Bill's front door. Bill noticed and started going down the ladder. But then the robot stopped at the base of the ladder, pushed it over . . . and Bill fell."

She shuddered. "He was all twisted up. I knew I wouldn't be able to do anything for him."

"But you still went over and took the robot?" Winston asked. "Why? It was evidence."

"No, it's a science project. One that earned Cam a full ride."

Winston shook his head in disgust. The blindness of an obsessed mom. But with his YouTube threat, he bet she'd spoken the truth.

Why had the robot come rushing out then? Had it been deranged? Winston doubted that. After all, it'd worked well enough to secure a scholarship. So the question was: Who had commanded Adom to push over the ladder? Who was the real killer?

# CHAPTER 33

WINSTON AND MARCY walked back home, Marcy lifting the robot high in the air like a trophy. Even Blueberry seemed to stroll along with pride. And maybe he should; the cat had kept the evidence from being snatched away after all.

Blueberry waltzed through the door like a king, into the kitchen, and paused in front of his dish. He acted like he was waiting for a reward. So Winston took out a can of salmon gourmet cat food from the pantry and gave it to Blueberry with a flourish. "Don't tell Kristy," he whispered to the cat. "She'll think I spoiled you." The cat wiggled his whiskers and started nibbling his food.

Smiling, Winston left the cat in the kitchen and joined Marcy in the living room. She'd taken over the futon and was lying across it, rotating the robot in her hands.

"How does this thing work?" she asked.

"Scoot over. I'll show you."

She sat up and gave him some space on the couch. "You were always better with machines."

Winston held Adom and peered at the robot. "If only so many different people hadn't handled it, then we'd be able to get the murderer's prints."

Or not. He'd tried dusting for prints last year (he'd had to Google how) and had ruined them.

Marcy peered at the robot's face. "What button do you press to turn it on?"

"Oh, it's voice activated," he said. "Bill showed me. It can do cool stuff like chop onions. Butler things."

"Neat," Marcy said. "I need one of those in my kitchen back home."

Back home? In London? Was she missing her life across the ocean?

Marcy interrupted his thoughts. "Do you think there's a command for it to remember the day of the murder?"

"Let me see." Winston stared into the robot's eyes and called out, "Adom."

A green light turned on, and the robot replied, "Ready for your command."

"Remember," said Winston.

Nothing.

"Recall," he said.

"Command unknown."

Winston gritted his teeth.

"Please try another action phrase." Adom paused. "Would you like a list of common commands?"

No, it would take too long to scroll through all the options. "There must be another way," Winston said, slamming his hand against the coffee table. A resounding clang echoed in the kitchen. Odd. Usually Blueberry moved around like a ghost, creeping back and forth from the kitchen to the rest of the house on silent paws. But maybe Blueberry had picked up on Winston's emotion, echoing it.

"Would you like to search for a specific command?" Adom asked.

"Yes." There must be a more efficient method of finding out what he wanted. What about a different command? One to push over a ladder.

"Search for *push*," he said to Adom.

"Push broom?" Adom asked. "First activated by user 001. Would you like to hear the entry?"

"No," Winston said. "Search for *ladder*."

"Ladder. Shove ladder," Adom said. "User 004."

"Hear entry," Winston said.

The robot spat out the recorded command. Winston recognized the voice right away, even though it had an edge of menace to it.

The kitchen door swished open all of a sudden, and the same voice of steel spoke. "Figured it out, did you?"

Winston and Marcy turned to look at Zack—and the gun he leveled at them.

# CHAPTER 34

WINSTON LICKED HIS lips. That didn't look like a BB gun in Zack's hands. "Is it *real?*" he asked Zack.

Zack grunted. "One hundred percent. Now hold out your hands, the both of you."

Marcy tried to work her charm on Zack by batting her eyelashes at him. "But I thought you said you'd never kill or hurt anything."

"I don't hurt animals," Zack said, "but people are a different matter."

Marcy wilted a little, and Winston figured the previous "crush" had all been an act on Zack's part. Maybe to cast suspicion off him. Or to get more info on how their investigation had been progressing.

Zack tied Marcy's wrists together and then proceeded to bind Winston's hands. Although the material was some sort of flexible natural fiber, it managed to cut into his skin, and Winston winced.

After checking the bonds, Zack tilted his head toward the kitchen door and said, "Now go in there."

*   *   *

As soon as they entered, Winston could smell it. Gas. The whiff of sulfur invaded his nostrils, and he could see the stovetop dials turned and the oven door wide open. Thankfully, Blueberry was nowhere in sight.

Zack commanded Winston and Marcy to stand side by side next to the range while he slipped on a gas mask. Then he linked Winston's right ankle to Marcy's left ankle with the tough eco-ties.

At least he'd die next to his sister, Winston thought, their feet bound together. But he needed answers before he succumbed to the toxic carbon monoxide. "Why'd you do it, Zack? And don't tell me it was for the gray water."

"Of course not." Even muffled by the mask, Zack's voice sounded harsh. "Bill had no respect for life, wanted to get rid of those sweet skunks. Little baby ones."

Speaking of devaluing life, Winston thought.

Zack continued, "He hired a company to kill that precious skunk family—"

"Oh, so you did argue with Bill about killing. Just like Heather said." Marcy took a swipe at Zack, but he moved away. Still attached to his sister, Winston almost fell over, but he recovered.

"The old man wanted to kill my friends," Zack said. "I took care of my furry buddies, checked on them every night."

"The video," Marcy whispered to Winston.

So Zack had gone over to Bill's place that evening, not to see about his neighbor's well-being but about the skunks' quality of life. It was no wonder skunks never left the neighborhood, with Zack taking care of them. Winston also guessed that the wild creatures had made that odd mewling sound the other night.

"I made sure to give them food," Zack said.

That circular object Anastasia had seen—Winston bet it had been a feeding dish.

"What do skunks eat anyway?" Winston asked. Maybe if he kept Zack talking, the man would make a mistake, and Winston could overpower him. But first Winston needed to free his hands. He tried to bite at his woven cuffs, but his teeth were too dull. (Less chomping on ice in the future, he noted to himself—if he survived this.) Plus, it would take forever for his incisors to sever the string, and the gas was spreading—in fact, he already felt a slight headache.

"Skunks eat insects, worms. They're absolutely essential to the ecosystem by keeping crops—even lawns—free of pests. Bet you didn't know that." Zack paused. "But I needed something easier to give them, so I fed them cat food."

Winston remembered seeing the large bag of cat food in Zack's home. He recalled Blueberry trying to leap over Bill's fence, too—probably to get a snack from the provisions left for the skunks. Just as he figured this out, a wave of dizziness hit Winston, and he tottered.

"It was the perfect crime," Zack said. "Old man falls off a ladder. I even erased the footage from his desktop. Nobody would have suspected, except then you had to get nosy."

"My brother was doing the right thing, you monster," Marcy said, but her voice came in slow spurts, like it took too much effort for her to talk.

"I erased all the evidence," Zack said. "Except I forgot about the recorded voice commands on the robot—until you, my dear, carried that blasted thing around the neighborhood like a trophy." Zack started coughing. "Huh, this mask doesn't help as much as I thought it would. Guess it's time for me to go."

Winston gulped. His sister had always bailed him out. He had to save her. While not dying. Plus, catch the killer.

He wondered if there was a weapon he could reach. Maybe something his free foot could use. But he saw only Blueberry's food bowl close by, and he still couldn't reach it to kick at Zack.

Zack unlocked the side door leading to the outside and stepped through. He leveled his gun at the gas range. "An explosion will burn up that robot. And get rid of you pesky meddlers at the same time."

Winston felt his stomach twist—and not just from the carbon monoxide. What could he do to stop the crazed animal lover?

# CHAPTER 35

WITH A GREAT cry, Winston bellowed, "Cat! We have a cat in the house."

Zack's eyes widened. "Oh no. That beautiful gray cat you were walking." He rushed through the connecting kitchen door to hunt the inner recesses.

Thankfully, he'd left the door to the outside wide open. A wave of air came in and refreshed Winston. "Now's our chance," Winston told Marcy. "Let's go to the living room."

"No, we should escape through the side door," she whispered.

"But then we won't be able to retrieve Adom. And maybe catch Zack. Come on," Winston said, gesturing to their tied feet. "It'll be like a three-legged race."

They managed to count off and walked *inside-leg, outside-leg* to the living room. Winston collapsed near the futon. How to get free? His eyes searched the room. The robot.

He activated Adom. "Cut rope."

The robot retracted its arm. Like during Bill's demonstration, it changed its limb to one with an attached blade. The sharp knife sliced through their restraints with ease.

Just then, Zack showed up with a wriggling and mad Blueberry in his arms. Winston did a speedrun and used the last of his strength to tackle Zack. Thank goodness he'd practiced catching Blueberry when the cat had tried to escape during their walk.

Unprepared for Winston's launch, Zack dropped hard. His gas mask fell off, and he groaned. Winston continued to pin him, his miniature Buddha belly helping to keep Zack down. Blueberry, now free from Zack's clutches, started clawing at his kidnapper's exposed face with all the vengeance of a furious feline.

Winston saw Marcy behind Zack cover her nose with her hand and enter the kitchen to turn off the gas. When she returned to the living room, she dialed the cops. He didn't loosen his grip (and Blueberry didn't stop scratching) until the police arrived.

*     *     *

It gave Winston a lot of satisfaction to see Officer Gaffey among the policemen who hauled Zack away. The cop shook his head at Winston, but there was also a glimmer of admiration in his eyes.

The police opened windows and doors to air out the house. Paramedics came to check on Marcy and Winston, but they both had no major injuries. Medical staff even evaluated Blueberry, who seemed insulted that they thought he'd need help.

That cat. Blueberry had saved Winston's life twice. First, Blueberry had been the reason Zack had gotten distracted and left. Second, chasing the cat had taught Winston how to really tackle and hold on tight.

"Come on, you rascal," Winston said to Blueberry, patting him on the head. "You deserve a treat."

After the kitchen had aired out, Winston went to the pantry and gave the cat another fancy meal for the day. "Lobster," he said. "Bon appétit."

He left Blueberry licking his chops and checked on Marcy. His sister lay sprawled on the futon. Winston didn't tell her to move over. Instead, he crouched down to her level and asked, "Are you okay?"

"Yes. No." Marcy furrowed her brow. "Almost dying makes you think about things."

"I'm sorry"—Winston put a hand on her arm—"I never meant for you to be in danger."

Marcy shushed him. "I came to you a mess. You wanted to draw me back to life, had me go investigating."

"But I almost got you killed."

Marcy looked at him and gave his shoulder a small punch. "Yeah, jerk."

He grinned, knowing he'd been forgiven. Here was the old Marcy—vigor mixed with a little spite. "What are brothers for?" Winston said.

Marcy settled into the couch and closed her eyes. "I'm exhausted," she said. "How do you do this all by yourself?"

"I didn't. I had Blueberry, and you, my dear Watson."

Marcy groaned. "Find another sidekick. I think I need to get back to my day job. Speaking of Watson"—she opened her eyes and gave him a probing look—"you know Kristy comes back tomorrow, right?"

He sure did. In fact, he'd been crossing the days off his calendar.

Marcy continued, "So much happened while she was away. Where would you even start?"

"Oh, I know exactly what I'm going to say." Winston gave Marcy a big wink.

# CHAPTER 36

WINSTON COULDN'T WAIT to see Kristy again, but he still had his sister pick her up from the airport. He hid behind the kitchen door, waiting for them to arrive. He felt himself shaking from nerves, either from the events of yesterday, or today's upcoming challenge.

Then the women entered the house, and Winston heard them chatting. Marcy filled Kristy in on the tragic passing of Bill and their solving of the case. (Marcy made sure to include her own prominent role.)

Kristy made approving noises, but at the end of the update, her sweet voice asked, "But I don't understand. Where's Winston now?"

At those words, Winston popped into their view. He sprinted over to Kristy—without even tripping over his own feet.

(Maybe he'd keep these new wingtip shoes to wear in the future instead of his typical flip-flops.)

Kristy's eyes lit up, and he thought she seemed to glow with joy. "You look great," she said. "Are you going somewhere?"

He'd swapped his usual T-shirt and shorts combo for a button-down dress shirt and slacks. Did it really make that much of a difference to his appearance? "No," he said. "I'm staying right here with you."

Her cheeks blushed a pretty pink. "You dressed up for me?"

He nodded and held out his hand to her. "May I have this dance?"

She complied, but whispered to him, "You do know there's no music, right?"

"Yes, but there will be." He gave a sharp look to his sister, who was busy staring down at her bare ring finger.

Winston cleared his throat, and Marcy sprang over to the radio to turn it on. Soon, strains of "Chances Are" could be heard.

As they twirled around the room (okay, bobbed), Winston told Kristy, "What I wanted to say during the Halloween party is . . . I love dancing with you. I'll always love dancing with you, especially to our song." He stopped mid-sway to snap his fingers.

Kristy looked at him, puzzled.

He snapped again, whistled, and then called out: "Blueberry!"

Still no cat appeared, so Marcy excused herself. She returned with Blueberry in her arms, and tears in her eyes. She set the cat down gently and left the room in a rush.

Blueberry strolled toward them. The cat looked particularly well-groomed because Winston had made sure to brush his fur smooth until it gleamed.

Kristy bent over her cat as he came closer to her. "Blueberry, you look so nice. Wait, what's this? A new collar?"

The cat was sporting a flashy sequined piece (not quite Tiffany's, but very bling). In the middle of the collar, instead of a tag, lay a ring. It also wasn't from the big *T* store, but given Winston's finances, it might as well have been.

Kristy's mouth dropped open. "Is that a diamond?"

"Sure is." Winston dropped down on one knee. "Will you marry me, Kristy?" His heart felt like a gong in his chest while he waited for her answer.

Kristy smiled at him. "Absolutely."

Woot! Winston swept her into his arms and clung to his new fiancée. He never wanted to be away from her again. When Blueberry purred at them, he swept the cat into his arms, too.

Moments later, Marcy entered the room with her suitcase. "Congrats," she said. "I'm really happy for you two, but I'll be leaving now."

"Where are you going?" Winston asked, releasing Kristy and Blueberry.

Kristy made a guess. "To London?"

"Yes, back home." Marcy looked at Winston. "You inspired me. To live—and to give love another try."

Maybe Marcy's brush with death had also changed her. Made her rethink things and soften up.

Then he got another punch in the shoulder from her. Okay, maybe not.

"Besides," Marcy said, "less chance of me trading my life for a skunk's over there."

Winston jabbed her arm. "Ha-ha. Hate to say it, but I'll miss you, sis."

"Me, too." She put her arm around his shoulder. "You're a good detective, and husband material," she said. "But I'm still the better D& D Dungeon Master."

Winston laughed and looked at everyone around him, including Blueberry. He gathered them into a giant group hug. Family. How much he loved each one of them.

# ACKNOWLEDGEMENTS

First off, thank you to all the Winston fans out there. Please leave an uber review wherever you can. Also, be sure to check out the Wong Pong game at www.jenniferjchow.com (under "Special Features").

Many thanks to my amazing editor, Linda G. Hatton! I'm also grateful to my ever-faithful critique group—hat tip to the SBW! Gratitude goes out to my family of origin, who had to listen to typewriting noise for years, including my big brother, the original DM.

And an epic thank you to my hubby and kids, who encourage, inspire, and give me space for my writing.